# NORTH DAKOTA
# NEIGHBOR

# North Dakota Neighbor

*A Novel*

### Marlene Chabot
### Author of *China Connection*

iUniverse, Inc.
New York  Lincoln  Shanghai

# North Dakota Neighbor

iUniverse books may be ordered through booksellers or by contacting:

iUniverse
2021 Pine Lake Road, Suite 100
Lincoln, NE 68512
www.iuniverse.com
1-800-Authors (1-800-288-4677)

Because of the dynamic nature of the Internet, any Web addresses or links contained in this book may have changed since publication and may no longer be valid.

This is a work of fiction. All of the characters, names, incidents, organizations, and dialogue in this novel are either the products of the author's imagination or are used fictitiously.

ISBN: 978-0-595-47893-4

Printed in the United States of America

This book is dedicated to my Norwegian neighbor, Andy Lee, and my friend Sue Poulin. Both loved life passionately and taught me many things while they were on this earth.

I wish to express my gratitude to Angie Sanders for spending her summer months editing my book. I also want to thank my husband, children, Eva, Sandy and her husband for encouraging me in the writing and publication process of my books.

On a cold spring morn, strangers met where the water's clash.
Mutual attraction was deep, but neither knew if it could last.
As summer flowers bloomed and faded, the two remained entwined.
Even wise words spoken by their elders didn't disturb them at the time.

But then the harvest moon hung in the sky, and the maiden shuddered for she was Sioux.
Her people would be gathering their belongings to return to the land they once knew.
Disheartened, her young lover fled believing there was nothing he could do.
Member of a different tribe, he was to remain loyal and stay where he grew.

After many moons came and went, the brave found the separation too much.
Twilight visions of the woman he loved were fleeing; he must get in touch.

Seeking counsel with the *"spirit world"*, he was advised to sever ties with his clan.
"Then you can roam freely, my son, searching for your loved one in an unknown land."

So he stole away quietly into the night like he was told.
Too bad his advisors forgot to share winter stories of old.

# CHAPTER 1

▼

"Father, it is good that you have left this world, for your weeping would cover the land. Our brothers and sisters have not hunted in many moons, not since they were bound to a land they did not chose."

I can definitely relate to that quote, I thought, as I continued to flip through the Native-American Indian calendar resting on my desk. My hunting has been stilled of late, and I've been fenced in for far too long. Heck, in my line of work, a guy should be offered at least one case a year that requires an out-of-town trip.

I feel like a lifer who knows he's never leaving prison but still blames someone else for his set of circumstances. Right now, I'm blaming Neil Welch, President of Delight Bottling for my inmate feelings. Why, before going to work for him it was perfectly fine for me to labor within the narrow confines of my abode. But then pow, along he comes, and I'm suddenly being jetted around the globe to bottling plants in Brazil and Germany, to name a few.

Yeah, yeah, I know I should be thankful to Mr. Welch for hiring me when he did. After all, I was in a deep slump before he arrived on the scene. Ah, let me correct that—perhaps I should be doubly grateful to him because once I resolved his problems he threw several of his cronies my way. But guess what? Not one of those elite clients required my expertise beyond the boundaries of Minnesota.

I'm not asking for much. Why, I'd be thrilled if I just got to drive east till I was an inch over the Wisconsin border—AKA cheesehead country or west across the state line for either of Minnesota's breadbasket neighbors, North or South Dakota.

You know, I often wonder if John Q. Public gives a fig about a small PI business owner feeling like a caged squirrel. Probably not. I mean why should he give a hoot. Well, even so, if I were asked, I'd tell him what a real day in the life of a PI was all about. It wasn't about good-looks or an excellent scriptwriter. Oh, the heck with them all. I'm going to chatter up one tree and down the next whether anyone wants to hear me or not.

Nuts! I just remembered no one has figured out a way to translate squirrel speak yet. I guess I could be nice and translate a shortened English version for you. A PI spends most days sitting behind a drab dilapidated desk doodling disjointed dribble drifting down dam phone lines; dumb dribble gets deposited in the dumpster, and then the daily digging begins anew.

Yes, stagnation reeks terrible havoc on this lone PI, and a case beyond Minnesota's borders is just what I need to invigorate my soul as well as my body. "Wait a minute! Wait a minute!" I brushed my hands through my hair and stretched my chair-sore body. A case that takes me out of town must also have real meat and potato substance, something I can sink these chops into. I stole a look at the calendar one last time, and then I began berating myself, "Stop daydreaming, Malone, reality calls." Next to the calendar sat a stack of disheveled papers I hadn't touched yet. Okay, what was so desperately crying for my undivided attention before I got sidetracked? "Ah, yes, the Harper case."

The sleazy husband ran off and left his wife holding the bag, the bag being six credit cards maxed to the limit, an emptied savings account, a colossal mortgage on the house, and three preschool aged kids. Sad to say, neither a pretty picture nor a unique story.

So far, since accepting the case, I had done minimal work on it—one, there wasn't much information to go on—two, the client didn't know how she was going to pay for my services; she wasn't one of Welch's beloved cronies. Yesterday morning, however, thanks to a phone number the missus provided, I finally obtained a smidgen of info on her elusive husband. I can tell you right now a smidgen usually isn't enough, but time will tell. I gotta admit one thing straight out, Brad Harper's one lucky fella in regards to relatives and friends; he has a total of six.

I probably should be frustrated by the lack of contacts, but it actually makes my next task a lot easier. This is where I gather all my notes and sniff through the information like a bloodhound or my crazy mutt, Gracie. Bury this one; doesn't make sense. Stash that one in a safe place for later. Ooh, yes, this one smells like a keeper—leave in view. Definitely do something with this one because ... well, you get the picture.

The fun part of my job really begins when the notes are done being sorted. I finally get to pound the pavement. A normal PI routine for tracing a skip case.

You know, no matter how hard the skips try to cover their trails, they always seem to slip up somehow. I mean, come on, have you ever heard of a slime ball attending a special school to learn how to be on guard twenty-four hours a day? I haven't. Well, Mr. Harper is no exception. According to the information staring up at me from the open folder, there's only one major difference between him and most of the people I've chased before: more educated. So he takes a little longer to screw up. Big deal. This PI will still arrive on the scene in nothing flat, tie up the loose ends and collect his fee.

I readied my hand to punch in a new number, but the ringing of the phone jumped in ahead of me. "Matt Malone, Private Investigator. How may I help you?"

"Hello." It was the soft, elderly Italian voice of Mrs. Grimshaw from the Foley Apartment complex where we both live. Now why was she calling, I wondered. She usually only disturbs me here at work when she's in dire need.

Panic instantly surged through my bones. I ignored my caller, for just a second, and dashed off a silent prayer to heaven. *Okay, God, you know the routine. Don't let this be a health-related call. She's already had her fair share.* When the prayer was completed, I reined in my concerns and tried using a lighter-toned voice, "So Margaret, how are you?" I kept my fingers crossed; I wanted to hear good news instead of bad.

"I guess I'm feeling as good as can be expected for a woman in her nineties." Hmm, her voice sounded weaker to me than it did a moment ago, but maybe it was my imagination. I held my tongue and waited. It was probably all of a micro-minute before a slight giggle passed through the phone lines, the kind of laugh a young child releases. My neighbor was definitely feeling fine. Luckily, her giggling didn't continue too much longer. "I just called to ask a tiny favor but an extremely important one."

Phew! I wiped the sweat from my brow. So the message wasn't of major significance, after all. Okay, God, I owe you one, real soon, maybe church on Sunday. The old gal probably just wants a ride to a church meeting or the grocery store. Since I knew my worries were unfounded, now, I reacted with less intensity. "What kind of favor, Margaret?"

"Oh, Matt, it's such a silly request. I need you to stop at Artie's Pet Store for me. Can you do that?"

That's it? I chuckled inwardly. What am I going to do with Margaret, the sweet old lady. She's always worrying about being such a bother. She doesn't realize the few things she asks of me barely cause a ripple in time. I finally answered. "Yeah, sure. What do you want me to get for you?"

Margaret spoke in a much softer vein now, what I classified as whisper level. Did she really think her neighbors might overhear her conversation? There's no way they could do that as the apartment walls are well insulated. Of course the ceilings and floors are another matter. "A box of bird food for Petey. I was going to get it yesterday, but then I went on an excursion for seniors and forgot. And today, well, my legs are too stiff to do any serious walking." Now her voice began to crescendo. "That darn shop till you drop senior outing. I would've been all right if we had stayed in the downtown area. But nooo ... they had to drag us to the Mega Mall."

"The Mega Mall!" I repeated. Just thinking about the mall's three floors of shopping experience gives me aches and pains; when I shop there, my legs give out before I reach the halfway point on the second floor. The poor woman. I understood her pain. "Would you like me to stop at the drugstore to get a muscle cream for your legs too?"

"Heavens, no! If you just get the bird food, this old woman, not to mention Petey, will be extremely thankful."

I sighed. Great! Now the dumb bird will like me even more, just what I don't need. "So what brand do you usually get, Margaret? As you know, I'm completely ignorant when it comes to birds."

"Oh, dear, of course you are, Matt. How thoughtless of me. I forget that you've never owned a bird, only dogs." The elderly woman's speaking voice quickly melted into mumbling mode. "Let's see, where did I put that empty box? Petey really liked that last brand of seed he had," then it faded entirely, followed by a loud clunk.

I wasn't concerned about the noise. I'd heard the familiar sound a thousand times before, a phone receiver hitting a hard object. But where the heck did my neighbor go off to? Was she still searching for the box?

Since I don't have call waiting, I hated tying up my business phone for non-work purposes, but what other option did I have? Haven't I always lived by the motto that it's down right rude to hang up on any person between the ages of seventy and one hundred. Now Sixty-nine, that's a different story. Come on, Matt, think positive, she'll be back in a second. In the meantime, what to do while the phones pressed against my ear. Ah, yes, check my hearing and see how many background noises I recognize before Margaret comes back: my reward—a fresh cup of coffee.

Okay, that's two points for the whistling teakettle and Petey's jabbering and an extra point for Margaret's rummaging through trash. Whoa! What's that? Someone other than Margaret is talking. I'm going to give myself four points....

By the time I heard my neighbor actually approaching the phone, my list of sounds was quite extensive.

It was another minute though before there was heavy breathing on the other end of the line. "Sorry to keep you waiting so long, Matt."

"No need to apologize, I found pleasant things to keep myself occupied with. So did you succeed in finding the box?"

My neighbor responded the way a person would who was distracted by someone or something. "What's that? Ah-yes. Yes, I found the box." A pause, then, "Good-bye Millie."

"Margaret! This is Matt. Have you forgotten already?"

The tone of her reply sounded like she was flipped out a of a hot frying pan. "Yes, I know who I'm speaking to, Mr. Malone. Just because I'm old doesn't mean my mind's not intact. Why do young people blatantly assume elderly people don't know what they're talking about?"

Mirrors aren't a part of the sparse decor in my office, but I was fairly certain my face just transformed from washed-out white to poinsettia red. Good thing my neighbor and I didn't own cell phones with cameras. Mrs. Grimshaw probably would have convinced me to head straight to the doctor to see about my blood pressure condition. I hastily repented, "Sorry, perhaps I misunderstood you. Didn't I hear the name Millie mentioned?"

"Oh?" she said in a more receptive mood. "Your comment makes perfect sense now. The doorbell rang just as I was setting the phone down." Ah ha! The phone was only dropped because someone named Millie stopped by. She took a deep breath and continued, "Millie's a longtime friend from the garden club. She came by to see why I didn't attend the meeting today. Such a dear! I asked her to wait while I finished a phone conversation, but she couldn't. She doesn't like being trapped in the afternoon traffic." Who does, I thought to myself. Margaret took another deep breath and changed the subject. "Oh, dear! I just realized the store might be out of Petey's bird food; it's happened before. Perhaps I'd better check with Artie, first, to see if he has the Kay-Tee brand in stock."

"Good idea," I said. "I'll just wait at the office till I hear from you."

My neighbor was slow to respond. "All right, Matt, I better let you get back to work. I've taken up enough of your time." At this juncture, the phones should've resumed their normal tones, but they didn't. Apparently Margaret wasn't finished with her side of the conversation yet. "Matt, wait!" she yelled across the phone wires, "Do you think I'm letting you off the hook that easily?"

"Huh? What do you mean?"

"Oh, come on. You know I enjoy your sharing a juicy tidbit with me."

"Sorry. Can't do it today."

"Why not?" she asked sternly. "You've done it before."

I twisted the phone cord around my short fingers. "I know, but I'm only working on one case right now, and it's still at stage one."

My words clearly irritated Margaret, for she hastily uttered, "Shoot," and then poof she disconnected.

# CHAPTER 2

▼

I'd finished my work at the office later than I had anticipated, but it worked to my advantage. Now I didn't have to sit for hours on end, tangled up in evening rush hour traffic along the Highway 65 corridor. And best of all, Artie's Pet Store was dead. I waltzed in, got the bird food, paid the bill, and exited within three minutes of my arrival time.

Five minutes later, I found myself in the underground parking lot at the Foley Apartment Complex. I turned the engine off, grabbed the pet food package from the back seat, slammed the car door, and headed directly for the stairwell.

I could've taken the elevator, but sometimes I preferred the healthy approach to reaching the fourth floor where I live. I lunged upward, two steps at a time, until I reached my final destination. Then I swung the heavy metal door open and walked down the brightly lit hallway to apartment 410: Mrs. Grimshaw's residence.

Just as I was about to let Margaret know that I had finally arrived, I heard a strange voice coming from her apartment. Hmm, is she entertaining a guest or listening to her television set? I leaned my mid-size frame closer to the door. I didn't recognize the second voice as a TV broadcaster's, but a two-way conversation was definitely being carried on. I wondered if I should return later.

As I contemplated what to do, the decision was made for me. My neighbor's door miraculously flew open. Startled, mouth agape, I struggled to say something coherent. Nothing came out, so Margaret took over. "Oh, it's you, Matt. Were you getting ready to knock?"

"Actually, I was debating whether or not to bother you."

"Why?"

"I ... er ... thought."

"Yes?"

"I, ah, heard you talking to someone."

"I was, so ...?"

The rest of the words finally tumbled out comfortably. "Well, I didn't want to disturb you if you had a visitor."

"Then it's a good thing my guest told me she thought she heard someone outside my door." No wonder she wasn't surprised to find me on her doorstep. "So are you coming in, or are you going to stand there all night?"

"Neither. I just planned to drop Petey's food off and be on my way; Gracie's still waiting for me, and I have a meeting to go to." I could tell by Margaret's facial expression that my reply didn't sit well with her, so I hastily added, "Tell you what, when I return I'll stop by for a short visit."

"You'll do no such thing, Matt." Margaret stared at me in disbelief as she fluffed the brightly flowered apron that was gathered around her tiny waist. "The dog can wait, and I'm sure that meeting isn't starting in the next two minutes. Besides," she said in a whisper tone, "I really want my friend to meet you," she fluffed her apron again. "She's a very busy woman and rarely stops by. You'd be doing me a huge favor."

"How's that?" I asked.

"My lady friends have begun to think you're a figment of my imagination because I talk about you so much and no one has ever seen you. Please stay and show her that you're not."

You know, if I didn't know my neighbor better, I'd swear she was trying to do some serious matchmaking. But that's so absurd. I mean, I've let her know how thick it is between Rita and me, haven't I? I made a hasty decision; a person can do that when they've learned through experience that it's best not to ignore an elderly neighbor's command. I stepped across the threshold and resigned myself to being introduced to whomever Margaret wanted me to meet.

I smoothly strolled into the living room with Margaret following close behind and discovered, to my surprise, an average built woman sitting so rigid on my neighbor's floral couch that she actually appeared frozen in time. She was wearing a sleek two-piece lime-green pant-suit. Being a PI, I noticed that her skin tones blended well with the couch. The stiff oval face she displayed, almost wrinkle-free, led me to believe she was in her late sixties.

Now Margaret allowed her colorfully-beaded-moccasin-slippered feet to take her closer to the couch to begin introductions. "Matt Malone, I'd like you to meet Claire Cox, a garden club acquaintance of mine."

First Millie and now Claire, I thought to myself. Good. It's nice to know Margaret has other people to check up on her besides me. I've always worried if I got hurt, then what. I graciously extended my right hand to Claire and stretched my mouth to form a grin. I really wanted to ask the *ice queen* if she was warm enough, but I didn't. "Hello. Nice to meet you Ms. Cox."

Margaret's stiff guest didn't reply verbally. She merely shook my hand and smiled.

Hmm … It seemed Margaret was left holding the bag, so to speak. Well, maybe her words will wake the frozen lady. "Claire, this is Mr. Malone, the man I'm always mentioning at our meetings." The visitor didn't seem to comprehend or didn't want to. My neighbor took another stab. "You know, dear, the man who looks in on me and occasionally runs errands for me." Wow! She finally displayed a tiny smile of recognition after which Margaret gave further information. "He did me a favor this afternoon." She pointed to the blue and yellow box still in my hands, "He purchased bird food for Petey. Wasn't that nice of him?"

Claire, the *ice queen*, finally decided to thaw. Too bad. The voice she projected was extremely nasally—like when you've got a rotten sinus cold. Perhaps that's why she was reluctant to use her voice in the first place. "Margaret is extremely fortunate, Mr. Malone, to have someone such as yourself to look after her."

Great! Margaret confused things once again. My face felt as though it was glowing like a red-hot poker, but it was too late to hide. I guess the only thing left for me to do was to straighten things out the best I could. "Just a minute," I pounced. "What Margaret said is inaccurate. I'm rarely asked to do anything for her. She, on the other hand, has done a heck of a lot for me over the years." With that said, the burning sensation in my face subsided considerably, and I figured I could safely change the topic. "So tell me, Claire, exactly how long have you and Margaret known each other?"

"Hmm?" The woman placed her right thumb under her double chin and softly pressed the bony index finger against her warm cheek. "Let's see. I've been a member of the garden club for about six years now, and if I'm not mistaken, you were already a member when I joined, weren't you, Margaret?"

Her hostess nodded. "Yes, that's right."

Claire continued, "We've been friends six years then."

I was getting ready to ask the woman another question, but then we were rudely interrupted by a loud squawking noise. It seemed to have come from one of Margaret's two bedrooms.

The noise appeared to agitate my neighbor, she swiftly glanced in the direction it came from. "Oh … I forgot all about Petey." Her head snapped back in my direction, and then she jerked the bird food out of my hands. "Excuse me, please, I need to tend to Petey. If I don't do it now, he'll be ornery the rest of the evening."

Claire and I chimed in, "Go ahead. Don't worry about us."

Margaret hastily removed herself from the living room and hustled down the hall to her spare bedroom where the screeching continued. "Squawk! Feed Petey. Squawk! Feed Petey."

Boy, I'll be glad when Petey starts eating, I thought to myself. His incessant speech was jarring my nerves. But then again, it sure made me appreciate my mutt more; give me a bark or a growl any day.

While the two of us stood helplessly waiting for Mrs. Grimshaw's reappearance, I stole a brief look at my watch. "Oops! Speaking of pets, I'd better get home and take care of mine. She can get awfully ornery, too." I slowly moved away from Margaret's visitor and began my leave, but right before exiting, I remembered the manners instilled in me as a child. I returned to where Ms. Cox still stood and offered my hand. "Sorry, I can't stay longer, Claire. It really was nice meeting you." Then for some unknown reason, I threw in an awkward twist besides. "Who knows, perhaps we'll run into each other again soon."

She cleared her throat. "Hmm, yes, one can never can tell, nowadays, can one?"

"Oh, and please convey to Margaret that I'm sorry I had to leave so abruptly."

The thawed woman gently squeezed my hand like she was testing a roll of Charmin toilet paper at the grocery store. "Why, certainly," she said.

# CHAPTER 3

▼

An hour had passed since I left my neighbor's apartment, and now my girlfriend, Rita Sinclair, and I were rushing to the northwest side of the metropolitan area to attend a special school board meeting which was to be called to order in approximately five minutes. We weren't interested in the meeting per se; we were only going there to act as distraction agents.

Let me clarify that. See, Rita's Uncle Harold, a board member, turned sixty today, and we were asked to keep him busy for a couple hours this evening. That request had come long before the board meeting was scheduled. It was his wife's idea. She'd planned a surprise birthday party and wanted the birthday boy away from home long enough for the guests to gather and hide. So Rita and I concocted a ruse. Harold was told we were taking him to a sports bar for a few drinks.

Rita and I entered the room at precisely seven and immediately gravitated towards Harold, to let him know we were there. After greetings were exchanged back and forth between the three of us, I positioned my head nearer to Harold and quietly asked, "Is this going to be one of those long, drawn out boring meetings or what?"

Before replying, Harold lifted his dirt-brown balding head and locked his olive-green eyes with mine. "Depends on how you look at it, Matt. Personally, I think you should be prepared to hold on to the seat of your pants. I've got this weird feeling there's going to be a heck of an eye-opener tonight."

"Really?" I thought it an interesting tidbit that Harold got weird feelings. So I hastily shifted my attention from uncle to girlfriend to see if she'd confirm the fact that he suffered from the same terrible curse I did: sixth sense—premonitions. When my eyes fell on Rita, she shifted her head from side to side. What type of an *eye-opener* is he referring to, then, I wondered.

Before I could work up the courage to ask, Rita slipped into the conversation. Chewing on one of her purple painted fingernails, she said, "Now Uncle Harold, we will be out of here by eight, won't we?"

"Oh, sure, sure, sweetheart," he loudly proclaimed as he firmly patted her free hand. "There will be plenty of time to celebrate my birthday. Don't fret." Then he pointed towards a tall, slender fortyish-woman standing at the head of his table. His voice took on a subdued tone as he solemnly added, "Carolyn Sorenson, President of Anoka-Hennepin's School Board. She's raising two elementary school-aged children single handedly, so she never allows the meetings to run overtime."

Just as Harold finished filling us in on the president, Carolyn Sorenson cleared her throat and announced in a crisp clear tone, "Everyone, it's time to begin."

Rita patted her uncle's hand. "I guess Matt and I better find a seat. We'll see you later." She dropped his hand and led me to the closest available table which ended up being near the back wall.

We barely positioned ourselves on unpadded card chairs when a loud resounding *whack* awakened our eardrums. The warning knock, made by Carolyn, was followed by instant silence. I leaned my bare elbows on the pine table in front of me and stared respectfully at the person controlling our behavior. Forget the body, Carolyn's straight, swaying black hair and the gavel she held in her good hand were persuasive enough.

"Good-evening," Carolyn began. "I'm glad everyone could make it. As you can see from our agenda, the main topic tonight is the middle school issue. Jennifer, would you start us off by reading the minutes from our previous meeting."

Since I wasn't in the mood to listen to a bunch of boring minutes, I escaped to the nearby hallway in search of a decent drinking fountain. When I finally returned to the meeting room, the secretary was sitting down, and Carolyn was preparing to speak again.

"People," she said in a commanding voice. "Our two existing middle schools are filled to capacity. A new school is desperately needed," she paused only a moment to pickup a sheet of green computer paper lying in front of her. With it in her grasp now she held it high in the air and said, "for those of you who don't agree, look at this latest home building projection. Two-hundred new students are expected to attend middle school next year. Are we going to require our teachers to use halls or bathrooms for classrooms so more students can be squeezed in? I don't think so. Remember, there are strict fire code regulations to adhere to." She rested the paper back on the table. "All right, that's all I have to say. The middle school issue is now open for discussion."

Harold's hand shot up first.

Carolyn took note. "Harold, you have the floor."

Harold stood and tugged at the bottom of his brand new, navy-blue J.C. Penney pinstriped jacket. "Thank you, Carolyn. Folks, she's right you know; we do need to be realistic. A new middle school has got to be built, but how can we, the board members, accomplish this goal?" Not waiting for an answer, he tugged the bottom of his jacket again and continued. "Homeowners in our district have already voted down a bond referendum and a tax increase, and the Minnesota Legislature informed us that there's no excess money available for building purposes." Harold's frustrations concerning the middle school topic soon became apparent to all of us; his body exposing him. Crossing his arms in a tight grip, he then said, "I don't know about the rest of you, but I think we're kicking a dead horse. Every time a new rock's turned over, we come up empty handed." With nothing further to add, he yanked his chair out and plopped down.

At the far right corner of the board members' table sat a pixyish woman with curly auburn hair. I only noticed her because she was playing with the nametag attached to her floral dress. Her hand finally moved, and I could see what name was being hidden—Mandy Miller.

Carolyn smiled at her briefly. "Yes, Mandy, go ahead."

The young woman projected a somber, mediocre voice. "Thank you, Carolyn. I, hmm, would like to propose a, ah, new very bold idea to the board. Hmm … I guess you could even say the idea is a little unorthodox." As she said this, the bodies around the main table stirred noticeably.

Carolyn, still standing, jumped like she had been jabbed with a needle. The minute movement threw her off balance just enough that she needed to grasp the corner of the table with her right-hooked hand. "What's this idea of yours, Mandy?"

"Hmm, well," Mandy replied, "I need a question answered, first. Are we allowed to, ah … request an enormous donation from just one individual?" Dead silence ensued around the board table. I suppose the members were probably all digging deeply into the recesses of their minds to find a comparable response.

Cindy Olson, a homely woman in her late fifties who reminded me of the wicked witch from the *Wizard of Oz*, was the first to break the quiet interlude, "Corporations loan money to the Minnesota charter schools all the time."

Harold scratched his head and then added, "I read that the Wilder Foundation gave a tremendous amount of money to help build a new type of school."

A petite, mousy-looking woman, Jennifer Johnson, quietly interjected, "Within this past year, I've read many articles pertaining to people who have set up special scholarships and endowment funds or have given money specifically to build gyms, performing art centers, and history wings, but all those gifts were given to secondary schools or colleges—not a middle school."

After a few more minutes elapsed and no other comments were forthcoming, Carolyn said, "I've been a school board member for roughly eight years, now, and I've never heard about any law that would prohibit a school district from accepting a large donation from one individual. If, however, the board wishes to delve further, for peace of mind, we can certainly check with our district's lawyer. Mandy, care to share who this new untapped source is you've thought of?"

"Evan Cox," she blurted out.

Now, even though I said I only made an appearance at this meeting so I could supposedly entertain Rita's uncle afterwards, I became extremely attentive after Mandy dropped the word Cox in our laps.

Harold was leaning back in his chair with his hands clasped neatly behind his head when he smoothly declared, "Ah—yes. Mr. Cox. I saw his name in <u>Minnesota Business</u> this past February. The magazine devoted an in-depth story to the top twenty-five wealthiest men living in Minnesota. Mr. Cox made the list. Is he a relative of yours, Mandy?"

"No, but my dad's known him since grade school. They attended old P.S. 101 together—the school that's on display at the Anoka County Fairgrounds."

Since Harold seemed to be the only other board member who had knowledge of Evan Cox, he played the devil's advocate. "Mandy, why would this Cox fellow want to donate money to building a school? It seems to me most millionaires spend their money on projects they know will bring them huge returns."

Mandy hotly defended Mr. Cox. "He's not like those other guys, Harold. He gives tons of money to charities, and I know he feels very strongly about the importance of a decent education."

Finally assuming her role as leader again, Carolyn stood and said, "Well, thank you, Mandy, for that remarkable suggestion. Now, how many board members think Mandy's idea is worth pursuing?"

One by one, hands slowly raised around the table until eventually all board members were accounted for.

Carolyn rubbed her chin. "Great, I think we've made an excellent decision. Of course we'll need some volunteers to create a speech that will charm the socks off Mr. Cox." A few hands went up.

"All right! Thanks for volunteering. I think three writers are sufficient. Now then," she tilted her short, midnight-black head of hair Mandy's way, "I think you should be the one to present the speech to Mr. Cox. After all, it was your idea."

Mandy's eyebrows arched severely. I suppose like the rest of us, she expected the president of the board to speak to Mr. Cox. "Ah, I guess I could do that," she answered reluctantly.

"Good," Carolyn said while stealing a look at her watch. "Are there any objections to the suggestions I've made?" The room remained silent. "All right then, I think it's time to adjourn. Someone please make a motion to do so."

Jennifer stretched and said, "Madame President, I move to adjourn the meeting."

According to *Robert's Rules of Order* Carolyn had to then ask, "Is there a second motion?"

I'll second the motion," Harold rapidly replied.

With the meeting adjourned, Rita and I rejoined her uncle. "Fascinating facts," I commented to Harold. "Being an apartment dweller for so many years, I never realized how tough it is for a school district to get help once homeowners vote down a tax increase. Do you think this Mr. Cox will actually rally around your cause?"

Harold glanced down at his black well-polished shoes that carried him down the hallway. "I haven't a clue, Matt, but I certainly think it's worth the effort."

As I silently held the main entrance door open for Rita and Harold to pass through, I remembered Margaret's guest. "Ah, Rita, did I tell you about the woman I met earlier today in Mrs. Grimshaw's apartment?"

"No," she somberly replied. "Should I be worried?"

"Of course not!" I nervously laughed as we approached my car. "It's just that her last name happens to be Cox. You don't suppose she's related to Evan, do you?"

"Nah," Rita and Harold answered in unison.

# CHAPTER 4

▼

## Beginning of August

Saturday is one of my favorite days of the week. It allows me the pleasure of wearing grungy clothes, playing with the dog and reading anything other than a PI manual, but I hadn't done any of those things yet today. I was too comfy hiding beneath the bedcovers to care about getting up or exposing my disheveled body to the showerhead.

Unfortunately, my lingering under the covers didn't last long. Gracie's great canine instincts told her I was awake. She immediately jumped on the bed and began pulling the blankets off of me, one by one. "Okay, okay, I'm getting up." I hung one bare leg over the bed then the other to show her I meant business. "See." As soon as both feet grazed the carpet, I stood and slowly made my way to the bathroom.

Normally I try to suds down as fast as I can, without leaving any soap residue on my body, because I don't believe in wasting water. I followed that same routine this morning and finished in mere seconds. Of course just as I turned the shower faucet off, the phone in my bedroom began ringing. I didn't waste my time trying to guess who was calling but rather asked myself whether it was worth the effort to rush out of there soaking wet. "Nope," was the hasty reply that floated from my mouth toward the fogged up mirror. Everyone knows bathrooms are one of the most accident-prone places in the home. The ringing continued. Obviously the person on the other end didn't agree with my safety concerns.

I reached for the towel on the door hook. "Ah, crap!" My clean towel was still in the hallway closet sitting on the shelf. I lifted the lid of the soiled clothes hamper standing next to the shower, dug out a towel and then wrapped it around my pudgy body. There, now I was ready to hear the voice of the persistent caller. I pulled the bathroom door open and took five giant steps across the light-tan bedroom carpet, leaving a trail of solid wet footsteps behind.

As I clutched the receiver I glanced at Gracie lazily stretched across the bed. Typical dog reaction, ears harshly peaked and eyes glaring back at the owner in an irritated fashion. Whoever said we don't really understand what our animals are thinking was dead wrong. I knew exactly what was running through this dumb mutt's head. *Get that darn phone. Can't you see it's disturbing my beauty rest?*

Guilt-ridden, I swiftly replied, "I'm getting it. Go back to sleep." On the first try, the phone receiver slipped through my wet hand and helplessly dangled from its cord. The second attempt was much better. I actually maintained my grasp and was rewarded when a cheery elderly voice greeted me.

"Good morning, Matt." It was Mrs. Grimshaw.

I hastily reacted as though Margaret might have x-ray vision and tested the tightness of my security blanket, the green-striped towel. "Oh, hello."

"Before you run any errands, do you have time to step across the hall?"

"Well, you're one lucky lady. It just so happens I don't have any plans for today. How about I slip over after I have a bite to eat?" I wasn't about to tell her I wasn't dressed yet. "Does that work?"

"Yes, that would be fine. Petey and I will be finished watching our game show re-run by then."

"Petey, your parrot, watches game shows?" I couldn't contain the laughter. "Ha, ha. You're joking, right?"

"No, I'm serious," my neighbor replied in a polite tone. "The bird and I have been watching television together ever since I heard Dr. Taylor, the renowned pet psychologist, talk on Joe Snyder's morning radio show. He said certain animals like Petey should watch television shows to keep them from getting lonely."

"I always heard adding an extra pet to the household helped with that. Why don't you buy Petey a mate?"

"Not on your life!" Margaret bristled with the conviction of a porcupine, "One Petey is all I can handle."

"Yeah, I hear you," I said as I ran my free hand through my wet hair. Petey can definitely be a nuisance at times, I thought to myself, but so can Gracie. "There's no way I could care for two dogs. I barely have time for one."

"Well, Matt, I'm sure glad to hear you say that because if you had two dogs you'd have to move to another apartment complex."

"Yes, and if that happened I also wouldn't get anymore great Italian cuisine from the good-looking lady across the hall from me."

"Three cheers for one mutt," Margaret said, her voice dripping with honey.

\*     \*     \*     \*

When I finally rapped on Margaret's apartment door, there was no response. I checked the doorknob, found it wasn't locked and hastily decided she was probably just in her back bedroom. So I waltzed in and loudly proclaimed my entrance. "Mrs. Grimshaw, I'm here."

"Matt?" The quick reply sounded like it was coming through a tunnel.

"I'm standing in your livingroom."

"And I'm in the bedroom," came her answer back. "Take a seat. I won't be long."

I hurriedly studied the room, and then I squeezed myself into Margaret's antique rocker, the piece of furniture furthest from the couch and Petey.

"Squawk! Squawk!"

"Don't worry. I see you Petey, although I wish I didn't." The dumb parrot had been perched on the top back part of the couch since I first walked in. Now he began to move towards me. "Whoa, Petey. There's no need for too much friendliness." I extended my right hand in front of me like a traffic cop standing in the middle of noon traffic. The bird ignored me. He continued to inch ever nearer. Looks like I only have one defense left to try. I lowered my voice and sounded as stern as I could. "Stop!"

At that precise moment, of course, the white-haired Mrs. Grimshaw entered the room. "Goodness sakes, Matt, does Petey still scare you?" He did, but how does one explain. "I thought you'd be over that by now," she said as she flapped her thin wrinkled hands out in front of me. "You really don't have anything to worry about. He won't budge from that couch till the show is over. It's his favorite one."

I didn't care what Petey wouldn't do. I just didn't trust the darn bird. As a matter of fact, whenever I saw him, memories from when I was a seven-year-old kid came back to haunt me: a warm summer day—Stanley Knox and his parrot. "The bird's harmless," Stanley said. "Just needs to stretch his wings." So of course we opened the cage and let the bird out. Everything was cool, too, until the dumb parrot decided to swoop down, land on my arm and tear some flesh away with its beak. My arm hasn't been the same since.

Ignoring what Margaret said about Petey, I immediately moved closer to her. Then I promptly gestured to the newspaper she held in her hand and asked, "What's that? Are you entering another crossword puzzle contest?"

"Yes, as a matter of fact I am," she answered, a bit too defensively. "This time I'm going to win. I can feel it in these old bones," and she patted her legs.

I lightheartedly replied, "You sure it's not just your arthritis acting up again?"

"That's not funny, young man. Weren't you ever warned about making jokes concerning elderly health issues?" Ouch, I didn't realize Margaret would take my comment so seriously. "You know, you've got me so upset now, I don't think I want to discuss anything with you."

"Oh, come on," I pleaded. "You know I was just teasing. Now what was it you wanted to tell me?"

A low laugh escaped my neighbor's aging lips, but it quickly grew in intensity. Wait a second! What's going on here? One minute the little Italian woman is very upset, and the next she's giggling uncontrollably. "I sure do love acting for you, Matt," she said. "I should've taken lessons when I was younger. Don't you think I would've made a darn good actress?"

"That was theatrics? You mean you were pulling my leg?"

"Afraid so," she answered. "but you deserved it young man."

I chuckled, "I suppose I did," and then I chuckled some more.

When the air finally cleared of laughter, Margaret explained why she invited me over. "Last night while trying to get to sleep, I realized it's been ages since I've had you and Rita here, and I want to remedy that. Do you think you two could come for dinner?"

"Ah, you don't need to have us for a meal," I replied. After I responded I realized my answer was too hastily said. My neighbor's face immediately pursed into a precarious position I recognized all too well. It's the facial expression that says—you've burst my bubble, buddy. I hastily rifled through my mind now for a simple cure to such a situation and discovered there was only one. "Er ... what I meant was, I've been wanting you to join Rita and me for dinner."

Margaret stabbed the still air with one of her arthritic fingers. "Nothing doing. Call me old-fashioned if you want, but I love entertaining, and besides I asked first. Who knows how much longer I'll be able to do it."

Well, that's true. Her comment made perfect sense, but many years ago I also learned you don't argue with senior citizens because you'll always lose. "So do you have a particular date in mind?" I asked.

My neighbor finally placed her newspaper on the laced-covered dining room table. "As a matter of fact, I do. Tonight or is that too short of notice?"

I placed my left hand at the back of my head before answering. "For me, no, but it could be quite tricky for Rita. Tell you what. I'll check with her in a little bit and get back to you." I dropped my hand to my side. "Now let me bring the dessert. Okay?"

"Fine," Margaret replied in her no nonsense manner. "I'll have plenty to do as it is."

# CHAPTER 5

▼

Margaret Grimshaw's sugary voice rang out, "Rita, Matt, you're right on time. Come in."

We stepped across the threshold like Siamese twins and entered my nonagenarian neighbor's charming abode. Rita shared a quick hug with Margaret, and when the women were finished, I presented Margaret with the white cardboard box containing the dessert.

She took the container from my hands and surveyed the contents of the box through the clear plastic part. "Thank you, Matt. Ooh—French Silk pie, my favorite. I'd better put this in the kitchen before I sneak a piece." Since Margaret needed to cut through the living room in order to get to her kitchen, she steered us in that direction. A variety of goodies were generously laid out on the coffee table. "Now you two help yourself to the snacks I've prepared. Dinner won't be served for another twenty to thirty minutes."

Wow! What a spread! My stomach had found food heaven. I immediately headed straight for the appetizers. But not Rita, my petite girlfriend. She ignored the stuff and strolled to the opposite end of the room and sat down. Resisting temptation is what women call it—another one of those things a female does from time to time. That's all right. You won't find men complaining about that. Heck, we appreciate the fact that our female companions watch their waistlines, there's more for us to eat.

I tilted my head toward Rita after I sampled a few things. She was staring out Margaret's apartment window—probably trying to keep her mind off the food. I stuffed another appetizer in my mouth. Boy I'm glad men have bottomless pits. We never have to worry about filling up before a meal.

While munching my way through a variety of vegetables, chunks of cheese, and crackers, my eyes slowly wandered to Margaret's dining room table. Flowers, wine goblets, fancy silverware. Whoa! The whole nine yards for Rita and me. Good china—five place settings. Five?

I was still analyzing the table set-up when Margaret rejoined us. "You don't mind another couple eating with us, do you?" she inquired in a timid fashion. Rita and I looked at each other, neither of us knowing how to reply. I think my neighbor picked up on our confusion. "Perhaps it would help if I said Matt already knows the woman."

Strong suspicions rang through the air as Rita's intense eyes raked me over the coals. Thankfully, she kept her lips sealed.

Trying to ignore the extremely strange look the woman of my dreams was giving me, I quickly swallowed the tiny bits of celery and carrots remaining in my mouth, turned to our hostess and swiftly asked, "Oh, and who might that be?"

"A garden club friend," Margaret replied. Now I want you to know that my eyes were wide open when she gave me her answer, but I'm almost certain they conveyed a 'nobody's home' appearance—you know, the dopey glazed look a dog gives his master when he doesn't want to do what the master tells him to. "Humph," Margaret grunted in an irritated way, "and they say us older people are forgetful. Matt! The woman was here visiting me only a couple weeks ago. The day you brought birdseed home for Petey. Remember?"

Lightning struck. I slapped my leg. "Ah, yes, the woman who told you I was at the door." Geez. How the heck did I manage to forget the frozen woman stuck on Margaret's floral couch, I asked myself. Ish! My head suddenly felt like a multitude of daggers were piercing it. Premonition time, I wondered, or was it just Rita's beautiful glaring eyes; they can be extremely lethal. I swiftly turned to see if my girlfriend was staring at the back of my head. Yup. I smiled meekly and shared one of my special looks which means, *Dear, there's nothing to worry about.*

Knock, knock.

Margaret's eyes danced with delight after hearing the sound at her door. "Wonderful, the other guests have arrived." She turned and went to let them in.

Even though we were alone again, my gal friend and I couldn't discuss the guest situation; the loud mingled voices in the hallway floating straight towards us would camouflage anything we said. That's why I chose to watch the minute hand on my watch instead and guess the exact moment the others would appear in front of us. I raised one finger, two fingers, three fingers.... It was time to stand.

Mrs. Cox recognized me at once, but then most women do. "Well, Mr. Malone, it's so nice to see you again." Sorry to say, her voice hadn't changed one iota since I last saw her; she still sounded nasally. Tonight, she happened to be dressed in a black cashmere sweater and full length black skirt—clothes just off the rack at Nordstrom's more than likely. "Oh, my. And to think we both thought we were just two ships passing in the night," she said as she fanned her flushed face.

Great! Another drama queen. Just what I don't need, someone more melodramatic than Margaret. I can't imagine where she got that two ships passing in the night thing, unless it was stolen from an old movie. I took a quick look at Rita and the elderly gentleman Mrs. Cox came with to see what their faces registered.

The presumed seventy-year-old male dressed in a light-blue wool sweater and brown knit pants, also reeking of Nordstrom's, merely feigned ignorance upon speaking. "Sorry, have we met before?"

I was about to reply, but then Claire Cox gently grasped the man's shoulder and said, "No dear. I met Mr. Malone a few weeks ago when I stopped by Margaret's."

The man's pale face turned pinkish. "Ohh ...?" His severe reaction kind of reminded me of a rabbit finding out he entered the wrong hole. But surprise, surprise, he swiftly went from embarrassed to a person who displayed great inner strength. He stole away from Claire's hold and stretched his aged-spotted hand towards me. "Hello, I'm Evan Cox. Nice to meet you, Mr. Malone." Ah, nice, I thought, at least his voice was in the normal range.

"Please, call me Matt, and it's nice to meet you too, sir." Wait a minute! The man said his name was Evan Cox. Rita grasped my hand hard. Apparently she just discovered what wavelength I was on. I gave her a slight smile. Yes, this has got to be the same man who was mentioned at that school board meeting. Hmm ... I wonder if Mandy has spoken with him yet.

Rita squeezed my hand again, this time I presumed to remind me that the introductions weren't finished. How could I have forgotten? Miss Manners would be terribly disappointed in me. "Ah, Mr. and Mrs. Cox, this is my girlfriend, Rita Sinclair." The three strangers shook hands, and then all four of us moved to the couch.

Now usually when Margaret entertains, she settles down in her favorite easy chair, the rocker, but it was empty and she wasn't occupying another seat. Hmm ... she must've snuck out to the kitchen when I wasn't looking. Well, since the hostess disappeared, I'll just fill in for her. "Evan and Claire, help yourselves to the goodies on the coffee table." They did.

Another ten minutes went by ... fifteen, and then Margaret announced, "Dinner's ready." When all of our plates were finally filled with thick juicy slices of roast beef, creamy mashed potatoes, fresh-cut green beans, and whole-wheat rolls, Mr. Cox got the dinner conversation rolling. "So, Mr. Malone, what do you do for a living?"

I stopped cutting my meat and rested the knife and fork on the plate. "I'm a private investigator, in business for myself."

Mrs. Cox chimed in, "Ah, and where is your business located?"

"Northeast Minneapolis—off of Highway 65 and Lowry Avenue." Now being careful to avoid any unwelcoming looks that would surely come, I lowered my eyes and continued. "The office isn't hard to find. Search for the one small decaying brick building that's situated on a corner surrounded by older homes."

As I raised my eyes, I noted that Mr. and Mrs. Cox shared some secret eye exchange with each other, and then their attention swiftly moved to Rita. Yup, as I had already anticipated, they wouldn't be interrogating me further. It happens all the time.

"And what do you do, Miss Sinclair?" Evan inquired in a barely audible tone.

Rita dabbed her pink-glossed lips with her linen napkin before she responded. That's what I like about her; she's the complete opposite of me. She's the cream of the crop, the *darling* of etiquette. As she placed her napkin back on her lap now, she said, "I work at a medium-sized advertising firm. Perhaps you've heard of it—Tuttles and Gray."

A huge smile enveloped Claire's face. Was it recognition or was she impressed? "Why, yes, of course, we know the firm. My son-in-law has had your company create ads for him. My ... that job must keep you on your toes."

"It does. Especially during the holidays," Rita replied.

Okay, now it's time for this PI to ask a few questions, I thought. I spread butter on my dinner roll and asked, "What about you two? Retired or still working?"

Mr. Cox, Evan, offered the answer. "Oh, we've been retired about ten years. Still very active in our community, though, aren't we, dear?" After his wife nodded in agreement, Evan clammed up. He was too busy playing *tug of war* with his sweater sleeve, now, to be involved in any kind of discussion. He must've spilled gravy on his sleeve, and was trying to hide it. I wonder who's going to win: the sleeve or him. Mr. Cox finally realized we were all staring at him. He stopped what he was doing, cleared his throat, and said, "Ah, Margaret, do you mind if I watch some TV? I'd really like to find out how the Twins did."

"Evan! Really!" Claire coldly declared. Her face was bright-red and contorted. "Can't you forget about baseball for one night?"

Margaret, known for her own apartment peacemaking skills, reached over and lightly tapped Claire's hand. "It's okay, dear. I don't mind. As a matter of fact, I'd like to see how the Twins did, too."

"Are you sure?" Claire asked in a softer, kinder tone. "Because Evan can wait till we get home to find out the results."

I eagerly stuck my nose in. "Oh, she's sure. Why, Margaret's one of the oldest baseball fanatics I know."

"For goodness sakes, Matt," Margaret scolded. "You needn't mention the word *old.*"

I stood, walked over to where she sat and gently pulled her chair away from the table. "Sorry," I said, trying to smooth ruffled feathers, "but you'll notice that I never said how old."

Rita didn't wait for my assistance. She took care of herself.

Mr. Cox quickly followed her example. He pushed himself away from the table and hastily retreated to the living room leaving his wife to fend for herself.

Acting dejected, Claire quickly cast her eyes downward, and then in a sarcastic tone, only audible for my ears to hear, she said, "Thanks dear! You always have to know how that darn baseball team is doing." Then she clumsily pulled her linen napkin off her lap and harshly disposed of it on the table.

Let me just say that was one awkward moment I don't ever relish repeating.

After the baseball widow was finished getting her feelings off her chest, I decided I didn't want the two of us remaining in the dining room gathering dust, so I sensibly suggested that we retire to the other room and see what all the fuss was about.

Mrs. Cox agreed reluctantly.

# CHAPTER 6

▼

When we joined the others in the living room, Margaret was still cradling the TV remote control in her right hand. She hadn't pressed the power button yet. Click! Now the TV finally came on. "Oh, Evan, look," Margaret said, giddiness dangling in her tone, "we haven't missed the results of the game after all."

"Wonderful," is all the elderly gent replied.

The local six o'clock news was only on a few seconds when the station broke for a commercial. Three minutes of ad time, then the newscasters returned, sharing the screen with an enlarged photo of one of Margaret's guests. Confused, I stole a quick look at Evan, redirected my eyes to the TV, and then revisited Evan's face once more. I'm sure Margaret and Rita did much the same.

What exactly was going on here, I wondered. But before I was able to analyze the situation, the station's perky blonde news reporter, Jane, squashed that idea. "Now here's an interesting story, Phil. It seems Minnesota philanthropist, Evan Cox, will donate land and money to the Anoka-Hennepin School District so a new middle school can be built."

"Wow!" Phil said in a surprised tone. "The parents in that district must be pretty pleased." He turned his head just enough, now, so it was facing the man seated to the left of him. "All right, Doug, you're up. What happened in the sports world today?"

The twenty-something sportscaster with dark, well-greased hair replied, "Not good news for the Twins I'm afraid, Phil. A big upset at the Metrodome where the White Sox beat the Twins, 9 to 4."

Our hostess couldn't control herself. She blurted out her inner thoughts, "Oh, dear, what a sad day for the Twins." She stood and ambled towards the TV to turn it off; totally ignoring the remote.

Hmm ... Margaret's lack of additional commentary threw me a curve ball. Normally, at this precise moment, Rita and I would be wishing we had cotton balls stuffed in our ears. I suppose I can excuse my neighbor for being remiss due to tonight's strange circumstances. I mean ... what a coincidence. Here we are, unbeknownst to us, watching television with one of Minnesota's richest men—when his picture suddenly flashes across the TV screen.

I leaned my head closer to Rita to reach her vanilla scented ear. There was something I needed to ask her, and I didn't want anyone else to hear. "Should we mention to Evan that you're related to a member of the board?"

My girlfriend didn't get a chance to answer. Margaret noticed us huddled together and began admonishing me. "Matt, remember your manners. It's impolite to whisper."

I swiped my fingers across the top of my hair while I thought of what to say. "You're right," I said. "Mr. Cox, Rita has information she'd like to share with you."

Rita immediately launched her cold peculiar stare at me—which interpreted means *I don't appreciate being put on the spot*—but she maintained her composure all the same. "Mr. Cox, I presume you've met Harold Sinclair?"

Evan shifted his eyes to the sleeve of his sweater which he began adjusting. "Yes, a couple times. We discussed details of the new school early this morning, as a matter of fact. A pleasant fellow. Is he related to you?"

"Yes, yes, he is," Rita acknowledged as she shifted her body on the couch. "He's my uncle. Perhaps you'd like to hear what he told my mother?" Evan didn't react, but my girlfriend continued anyway. "The board members are extremely pleased by your generous donation."

From the looks of things, Mr. Cox was obviously a humble guy. He didn't beam from head to toe like a proud rooster. Instead he quietly bent his head and clasped his hands.

We all seemed to be in perfect harmony with Mr. Cox as we basked in utter silence for several minutes together. Eventually the peacefulness was broken by me when I quietly asked about the building project. "So when will construction begin, Evan?"

Evan raised his fit body off the couch, stood, and crossed his hands behind his back. "Before the actual digging can start, a PERC test has to be taken. Drainage conditions are pertinent to the approval of the location." He then cleared his throat and allowed a tiny grin to shape his face. "A school doesn't have just one or two bathrooms like our houses, you know."

I laughed. Not only was he rich, he also had a sense of humor, too.

Smiling generously, Margaret daringly intruded. "Evan, dear generous man, what a wonderful gift you've given the Anoka-Hennepin School District. I only hope the parents appreciate what you're doing for their children."

Wife Claire, probably not wanting to be left on the sidelines any longer, shared her thoughts. "Oh, I'm sure they do Margaret, especially since their taxes won't be raised one tiny iota," she squeezed two of her fingers together.

All of the sitting was making me antsy. I stood and strolled over to where Margaret was resting comfortably in her rocking chair. "Evan, correct me if I'm misinformed, but didn't the school district already have land set aside to build on?" Rita and Claire both looked at me quizzically, as if to ask where I was going with this line of questioning.

He hesitated for only a moment, but that was enough time for Margaret to cut in. "Ah, I see what you're getting at, Matt. School districts generally reserve land for future use." She turned to her friend the philanthropist and asked, "Why did you donate your land then?"

Evan moved smack dab in front of Margaret's rocker. He looked more alive than he had since he'd arrived. "The school district does have donated farmland waiting to be used, but after checking out the site, I felt the district was better off with my larger piece of property. Plus, the land's enormous pond and wooded area make for a great nature preserve, a perfect setting for science classes, wouldn't you agree?"

I wasn't sure how to respond, not being a whiz kid in science. Thankfully, the light of my life, Tuttle and Gray's super marketing genius, took care of the situation quite nicely. "I suppose the school district will put the other property on the market then—so there will be money to purchase more sophisticated lab equipment and such?"

Mr. Cox spun his body half-way around, facing Rita head on now. "I hope not. I told the board that they should save their other piece of land for future needs. The boundaries of the northern suburbs are expanding at a phenomenal rate. Everyone wants a piece of the pie when it's a decent distance from the downtown area."

A loud yawning sound erupted quite suddenly from Claire. Either she was extremely bored with our discussion or she was really tired. Whatever it was, she succeeded in getting our attention. The three of us fell mute. At first, Claire seemed bewildered by the silence, but then she pushed her body off the couch and flatly announced, "It's late, dear. We really should go." Her husband swiftly obeyed and returned to her side.

In the meantime, I quickly stole a look at my watch: almost nine. Rita and I should make our exit, too. "Ah, Margaret ..."

My neighbor held up her tiny hand. "Don't say a word. You're all abandoning me at once."

"Afraid so," I gently replied as I moved towards Margaret's other guests and shook their hands for a second time. "It was nice spending time with you two. Hopefully our schedules will be clear when the school's dedication ceremony takes place. We'd really like to be there. Of course, Mrs. Grimshaw can catch a ride with us."

"Good," Evan said as he plunged his right hand into the lower pocket of his suit jacket, "but the ceremony won't be for at least a year."

"Dear," Claire said, "you're forgetting about the groundbreaking ceremony. That's fairly soon, isn't it?"

Her husband yanked his hand out of his pocket and displayed a handsome amount of keys between his fingers. "You're right. Thanks for reminding me. Naturally, the public's allowed to come to the groundbreaking ceremony, too. It won't last long, but it sure would be nice to see a few familiar faces."

Rita, Margaret and I responded in chorus fashion, "We'll certainly see what we can do."

# CHAPTER 7

▼

**Beginning of September**
**Groundbreaking Ceremony**

A thin, devilish grin decorated Evan Cox's face as he rose, left the six seated Anoka—Hennepin School Board Members behind and gracefully approached a dark wooden podium. He seemed to have gained new height today, but that was just an illusion created by the three foot riser he was standing on.

Rita and I still lingered by the first shovelfuls of rich black earth that were tossed only seconds ago. We thought the spot where we were standing was fine, until someone decided to test the microphone. The sound that carried to our ears wasn't good. So we did what anyone else in our shoes would do, we played field mice and scurried closer to the stage.

Once we arrived at our new location, we discovered there was no reason to have rushed there, after all. The generous benefactor for the new school didn't begin his prepared speech right away. He stepped sideways, first, and spoke to the people behind him. "Carolyn, thank you for that kind introduction. Board members, thanks for soliciting my help in raising funds for the new middle school." Then he quickly straightened his body and faced those of us on the ground. "Good-morning, ladies and gentleman. Glad to see the chilly weather didn't keep you away, but I still have bad news to share with you. My speech for this event is extremely short, so if you were expecting to hear a lengthy one, you'll have to return for the dedication ceremony."

Several listeners chuckled, myself included.

"So here we are, this little community, preparing to build a school when other small town schools are closing. Isn't life strange! Today, you and I are witnessing the start of a great event for the town of Oak Grove." People clapped. "Since the school is such a key element of a community, it's only natural for the community to gather together to celebrate the school's birth." Trying to be heard over more clapping, now, Evan inched closer to the mike and raised his voice a couple notches. "Many studies have shown that wherever a school exists, a town prospers; a unique partnership forms between the students and the community. Students take on projects for the betterment of their communities, and the communities take pride in the student's accomplishments.

"A politician once said that schools were formed so youth could throw off their 'robes of ignorance'." Mr. Cox suddenly jarred the podium with a forceful blow. "Well, folks, if we don't continue to provide the necessary schools, our youth aren't going to be throwing off any robes." Boy, he hit the nail on the head, I thought to myself, and the audience obviously agreed too because they gave him a thunderous applause. I suppose he would've gotten a standing ovation, besides, but we were already standing.

Mr. Cox sure kept his word. His speech lasted five minutes at the max. You'd never know it by Rita and me though because we were chilled to the bone. Of course, if it hadn't been for the unusually strong September breeze and the proceedings beforehand, I think we would've been all right. Poor Rita. Seeing her clutching her elbows tightly together reminded me of the many winter walks I took, back and forth between home and school, as a child. We'd all snuggle our books against our chests so they wouldn't have a chance of dropping on the ground and getting damaged by the mounds of snow covering the sidewalks. There was no way we were going to be chastised in class the next day by the nuns.

My nose started dripping again for the umpteenth time, and so I hastily retrieved the handkerchief stashed in the front breast pocket of my blue suit coat and blew my nose. Once that was taken care of, Rita and I entwined our arms so we could share body heat, but her fall jacket was impeding the process. Darn! If it weren't for our wanting to say hello to Harold and Evan, we could've been in the warmth of the Topaz by now. "I don't feel any pangs about the brevity of Evan's speech. How about you?"

Rita opened her mouth to reply, but unexpected shouting cut her short.

"What the …?" I quickly spun Rita and me in the opposite direction.

A short, squat, balding guy, clothed in work jeans, a long sleeved blue-faded shirt, and scuffed black safety shoes was plunked firmly in the sand, his back to us so we couldn't see his features. He yelled again, and this time I caught what he was saying. "Ron! I said you can let her rip. So get moving!"

The muscular man seated high above us in the cab of a Cat tractor let loose with a loud whoop as his excavating machine roared to life.

The guy that I presumed was Ron's boss took the fastest giant steps backward I've ever seen. He just barely missed crunching Rita's size-seven feet only because I realized what he was about to do. I quickly stretched my arm straight out placing it between the two of them. Then in a loud voice I said, "Hey! Watch it! There are people behind you."

The stranger immediately turned to us and apologized in a gruff manner. "Sorry, didn't know anyone was around me."

"No harm done," I assured him as I stole a look at the name emblazoned on his shirt pocket. "You stopped in time, Stan. What's with the guy you were yelling at? He seems to be overly zealous about his job."

"Him?" He pointed to Ron. I nodded. "He is, but you would be too if you were sitting in a cab that changes to a hell of a hothouse as the day wears on."

His comment in regards to extreme heat in the cab took me by surprise. "Aren't all those big rigs air-conditioned?"

"Nope, not all," he replied pleasantly. "Unfortunately, the older machines in our fleet don't plan to drive off to machinery cemetery anytime soon even though our guys wish they would." Now he pointed at Ron again. "See his forehead mister. It's perspiring, and it's not even noon." I pulled my shirt sleeve up to check the time: eleven-thirty.

Rita took advantage of my actions to wriggle free from me. At first I thought she just didn't need the extra body heat anymore, but then when she swiftly clasped her hands together above her eyebrows, I realized a homemade visor was just taking top priority now. It could shield her eyes from the sun's harsh glare. "Phew. I can only imagine what he feels like at the end of his shift," she said.

"Lady," Stan roared, "you have no idea. At the end of the day he's completely drained, and all a guy like him wants to do is sit in some easy chair and toss back a couple beers."

"How long do you think it'll take to complete this project?" a deep-serious voice shouted from behind us. The voice belonged to Harold Sinclair. He must've made his way to us while we were distracted. "Seems like the last time your company built a school for us, it was completed way past the promised date."

With Harold's arrival, Rita and I finally turned in the direction we originally intended to go.

Mandy Miller was just coming up alongside Rita's uncle. She reminded me of a cat, the way she stretched her dainty body and purred, "Harold, don't bother the work crew. The engineer in charge already answered your question at our last meeting. He said the job will be completed on schedule. If not, well, he knows a huge sum of money will be deducted from his company's payment," she said as she licked her lips clean.

Stan didn't respond to either Harold or Mandy. He merely dusted the bottom of his pants off and deserted us; so much for the boss sticking around.

I guess it didn't matter that he left. He couldn't answer the one question I had, anyway. "So when do you expect the teachers to move into their new digs, Harold?"

Before he answered me, he created a visor similar to the one Rita created earlier. "Probably by October of next year."

"Has the board selected a name for the school, yet?" Rita asked as she raised the collar of her jacket and held it snugly against her neck. Hmm, she's already forgotten about the body warmth we shared with one another, and I'm getting colder by the minute.

Harold Sinclair's olive-green eyes quickly shifted from his niece to Mandy.

"Go ahead," his cohort said, "tell them. I'm sure they know how to be discreet," she licked her lips again.

Rita's uncle lowered his monotone voice a notch. "Well, the consensus reached at our last meeting was to name the school after its benefactor—Evan Cox."

Only gleaning a teeny bit of knowledge concerning school names, recently, I hesitantly commented, "I … that is … I thought schools were just named after famous dead people." I automatically ran my hand across my smooth chin. "That settles it, Rita. We're definitely going to the dedication ceremony. Heck, it's history in the making—a school's being named after a person we actually know."

My girlfriend finally released her jacket collar. "Uncle Harold, you will remember to give us early notice of the date for the ceremony, won't you? Matt and I have such crazy schedules, and we need to mark our calendars way in advance."

"Yes, of course, dear," he replied. "I promise I won't wait till the tenth hour to tell you, like you two did on my sixtieth birthday. By the way, what happened to Margaret? I thought she was coming with you?"

"A wee bird crisis," I said directly to Harold. "Petey swallowed something he shouldn't have." As I completed my sentence the corner of my left eye caught movement where Mandy was last seen standing. Curiosity bit my tail. I now focused all my attention in that direction. Hmm, what have we here? A sleek, burnt-auburn cat in high heels was running faster and faster to catch its prey: Evan.

# CHAPTER 8

▼

**First Week of October**

"Mrs. Harper, this is Matt Malone. I haven't caught you at a bad time, have I?"

Violet Harper yawned into the phone. "No, not at all Mr. Malone. I was just filling out my millionth job application. Have you found that darn scoundrel I used to call my husband?"

"Er, no. But I am calling about him," I said in a gentle tone trying to calm her down. "I thought you should be brought up to date."

"All right. Go ahead I'm listening."

Great! I got her to pay attention to me, and now I'm not quite ready to talk to her. "Ah, Violet, hang on one sec." I scooted to the farthest edge of the couch to retrieve a folder I had left on the cushion. Of course, at that precise moment, Gracie hastily took advantage of the newly available space. I tried to shove her off the cushion, but she did all she could to remain firmly rooted, even going so far as to make sure the furriest part of her head was plopped in my lap. That's it! "You nutty dog, get off the papers," I scolded.

"What was that?" I heard Violet inquire. "Mr. Malone, I didn't quite catch what you said."

Thank goodness! I couldn't afford to have Mrs. Harper think she'd hired a crazy PI. With the dog out of my way now, I picked up the phone again. "Ah, I just called to tell you the latest list of phone numbers you gave me hasn't generated any leads yet."

"Hmm ... I was so sure one of those people would've known something. Evidently my husband hasn't contacted anyone since he skipped out on me," she started weeping into the phone.

If there's one thing I can't handle, it's a crying woman. I'm a real sucker when it comes to teary-eyed ladies. "Ah, don't give up just yet, Mrs. Harper. My gut feeling says your husband never left town. As a matter of fact, I think he's going to surface here real soon." There, that lie ought to help pull her through, I thought.

Violet blew her nose into the phone so hard people a mile away could've heard her. "I hope so, Mr. Malone. In the meantime, I guess I'll just keep going to job interviews and hope someone will take pity on a forty-year-old woman and hire me."

Not knowing what else I could possibly say to cheer her up, I simply added, "I promise to call you the minute I get wind of anything. Oh, and good luck with your job search, Mrs. Harper."

"Why, thank you, Mr. Malone. It's kind of you to say that. Good-bye."

"Good-bye," I repeated. When I placed the phone back in its cradle, I was reminded of something Rita and I had recently discussed. Men who want to vanish off the face of the earth have it much easier than their women counterparts; besides dying their hair and wearing wigs, they can add beards, goatees, mustaches, and sideburns.

Enough thoughts about Mr. Harper. I placed my hand on the miniature calendar resting on the coffee table and tore the September sheet off. It was now October or Indian summer, whichever you preferred. Soon leaves of every imaginable shape would be dropping to the ground in bucketfuls; squirrels had already begun harvesting their nuts. For Minnesotans, October weather is the best kept secret. It's like finding a pearl in an oyster. "Then why don't you do something fun outdoors this weekend?" I asked myself.

Gracie immediately pulled herself from her reclining position. I rubbed her head. "Do you think Rita has plans for this Saturday?" The mutt twisted her head from side to side. Poor girl, she didn't understand my question. "No, she's not here." Oh, heck, why did I even bother asking the question. If Rita doesn't have to work, she's probably already got something brewing with her girlfriends. "Still, it could be she doesn't." I think I'll just check and see what's happening around town and then give her a jingle.

I reached for the week-old Sunday paper that was partially hidden under a cluster of magazines that the mutt's butt was covering. Of course, true to form—Gracie wouldn't give an inch. She was continuing her stubborn streak this morning. Time for the old "mind over food" power game, I guess. I dug in my bathrobe pocket for the Milkbone biscuit I had forgotten to give her earlier. I could use it now for bribery. As soon as she saw what I had for her she stood and snapped it out of my hand freeing the paper and magazines.

There was nothing of interest on the entertainment section's first three pages, but a tiny ad on the fourth page managed to draw me in. A Fall Heritage Festival (a mini-Rendezvous) was planned for the upcoming weekend. It would be located on the east side of downtown Minneapolis and would cover the whole Old St. Anthony Main district: by the lock and dam and the Mississippi River. I was ecstatic. Since touring historic Williamsburg in the early 70's, I'd become deeply intrigued by the early history of the United States: especially Minnesota's. I even go so far as to envision what life would've been like for me, say circa late 1700's or early 1800's.

Oh, I've seen myself as a voyageur—traversing the mighty Mississippi River. In another daydream, I've traveled with Sir Du Luth to search for the shortest water passage to the Pacific Ocean. Most of the time, though, my visions merely portray me as a foot soldier parading up and down the grounds of Fort Snelling. Imagine the excitement then, when I first discovered that history buffs from all walks of life actually gather at what they call a Voyageur Rendezvous. On selected weekends, they reenact the lifestyle of a bygone era such as that of a fur trader's life.

Whoever selected the upcoming Heritage Festival site couldn't have picked a better spot. Books on Minnesota history state that the Ojibwa Indians were the first people to use that land by the falls and dam. In the late 1600's, Father Hennepin, a missionary priest who was captured by the Ojibwa Indians, was brought to the water's edge to observe a buffalo hunt. Much later after his release, he wrote about the beautiful waterfall he had seen and named it after his patron saint, Saint Anthony. Of course, the famous flour mills which were eventually clustered along the nearby banks didn't begin popping up until a century later.

Okay! I've got a plan. Now I hope Rita's available. I punched in her private work number and waited. Come on, please be there, I thought. The phone rang—once, twice, three—.

Finally, a breathless honey-dewed voice said, "Hello, Rita Sinclair speaking."

"Hi, hon. I hope I'm not interrupting anything."

"Actually, you have good timing, Matt. I was just getting ready to leave my cubicle to get lunch, but that can wait. How you doing?"

"Not really sure." I twirled one of my many Bic pens in front of me. "I'm not making any progress with one particular case, and it's bugging the heck out of me. I thought maybe if I cut loose from the office, for just a day or two, it might help. As a matter of fact, that's why I called." The pen I was fooling with quietly slipped through my fingers and fell into my lap. "What do you think?"

"About playtime? I guess it couldn't hurt."

"Really? Geez, that's exactly what I was hoping you'd say. Care to join me Saturday?" I questioned. "That's, if you've haven't got something better planned."

Rita's tone became highly animated. "What do you have in mind, Mr. Malone?"

With my free hand, I picked the pen up and set it on the coffee table. "Do you remember my telling you about that Rendezvous I attended last year?"

"Yes," she laughed, "that's something I won't soon forget. You spent the whole evening talking about nothing else."

I pushed back the hair that had been covering my forehead. "Oh, sorry, I don't remember that part, but how would you like to go to an 1800's gathering with me?" I asked. "Even though it's not a full-blown deal, I'm sure you'd still enjoy it."

"Sure," Rita cooed. "Might as well make the most of the sunny weekend we're supposedly getting."

Yes! I lightly tapped my hand on the coffee table. "Great! I'll call you later with the details."

The speaker part of my phone piece was just about to meld with the receiver when Rita yelled over the lines. "Matt! Wait! Do I need to wear clothing from that era?"

I laughed to myself. Picturing Rita in anything but two-piece suits, an occasional evening gown or jeans didn't work for me. "Hey, if you feel inclined to go that route, do it. Me, I've never had the nerve."

# CHAPTER 9

▼

It was devilishly warm by the time I picked up Rita and pulled into the parking lot on the northeast side of the Third Avenue Bridge. The temperature was seventy-five degrees and rising. Since it was almost noon I was having trouble finding a parking spot for the Topaz, but did I blame the time of day for our problem? No. I chose the nice weather instead. It wasn't until I had driven down the third lane in search of an open slot that I began chastising myself for not coming earlier like I had originally planned. Of course, my whining didn't stop until I found the perfect place to stash the car.

With the car finally parked, the two of us climbed out of it sporting matching navy-blue-jean attire. My girlfriend had decided she wasn't quite ready to transform herself to the 1800's either.

Rita shook her tiny head. I had no clue what that was about until she spoke. "Geez, the quietness is spooky, Matt." She was right. From our vantage point, at the trunk of the car, it appeared that nothing was going on in this part of town, but I knew better. "You sure you got the date right?"

"Yes." I waved at the rows of cars sitting in the parking lot. "Would all these cars be parked here if nothing was happening? Wait till we get near Pracna on Main. There'll be tons of activity, you'll see."

As usual, I was right. Once the rubber soles of our tennis shoes meshed with what remained of the old, rusty-colored cobbled streets, St. Anthony Main came alive—every type of vendor was now vying for our money. I tuned them out, my girlfriend wasn't able to.

You're probably thinking I was indifferent to the vendors solely because I'm a male. To that theory, I say, "Hogwash!" It's because, as a PI, I'm in constant filter mode. For instance, across the street from us right now an 1800's encampment group was being forced to scatter due to over zealous 20<sup>th</sup> century onlookers. I gently tugged Rita's hand to let her know I preferred to move across the street and leave the vendors behind. Sweet gal that she is, she instantly complied to my desires, or so I thought.

When we finally reached the campfire, where some of the crowd happened to be gathered, Rita slyly slid me some info. "Those shopping bags from the Minnesota Historical Society store sure are a sharp marketing tool." I nodded agreement, thinking she simply had work on the brain—being in marketing. Of course, I should've realized there was more to it than that. "Matt, maybe we could check the place out. I bet they've got copies of today's activities and schedules for the trolley ride."

Not thinking about the words that next floated across my muscular lips, I merely replied, "If that's what you want to do, dear, I believe the store's only a block from here." With that said, I temporarily sealed my lips and drew my attention back to the giant flapjacks being prepared over the open fire. It didn't take long though before the pancakes were ready to be shared, and at that precise moment my lips parted again. "I'm sorry, Rita, did you want to go to the store right now?"

As she answered, "Yes," she displayed a huge grin. Nuts! The clever gal hoodwinked me yet again. We quickly hooked our hands together and slipped away from the crowd.

"I can't believe this trolley tour has been operating two years already, Rita."

"Why would you remember something as trite as that?"

I combed my fingers through my hair. "Because I happened to take a trolley tour of downtown Key West about a year before the trolley rides started here." I paused.

"And, go on," Rita prompted.

"Well, the concept was so impressive, I actually thought of copying the idea for the Twin Cities scene. Too bad I didn't talk to someone in the industry as soon as I got back home, but I didn't figure on anyone beating me to the punch. As the French say, *C'est la vie.*"

Rita's new destination for us was unfolding in front of us now. Four long tables piled high with history books sat adjacent to a store that was waffled between two empty historical buildings. The sale sign wafting in the light breeze immediately hissed at me. "Hey, buddy, come and see what we have for you."

"Ah, Hon," I said as I released her hand, "I think I'm going to browse for a second or two. Why don't you go inside, ask about the tours and get a program for today's events." I didn't think she'd mind taking care of that stuff since it was her idea to come to the store.

"Okay, but don't get so engrossed in the books that you forget I'm in there."

"I won't." Hmm ... what have we got here? Books on Native Americans of Minnesota: Ojibwe and Dakota. A few of the books were actually written by Indians rather than by European descendants. That could make for interesting reading material, I thought to myself, as I picked up four books and continued to shuffle through the rest. Beep! The timer on my watch went off. I guess I'd better decide which books I really must have. A tiny voice lurking in the back of my head swiftly replied, "Get the book about the Dakota Indians." I took the message to heart, placed the rest of the books back on the table, and went to search for Rita.

No line at the check-out counter, but also no salesperson. As soon as I turned to view one side of the store, I spied Rita standing by a magazine rack. She caught my eye and immediately left what she was studying to join me at the cash register.

"Hey, look what I found," I said like a teenager who has just found his precious bag of marbles after being lost for many years. "Just don't ask why I'm buying it." No sooner had those words tumbled out of my mouth then queasiness invaded my entire body. I recognized the symptoms right away so for protection, more than anything else, I hastily latched on to the edge of the counter hoping the crazy nausea would diminish rapidly. It didn't. My upper extremities now began inching their way toward the worn out Maple-planked floor. While I continued in a downward-slide position, I tried to picture what might be racing through my girlfriend's head. "Matt's in his forties, and he's a little overweight. Oh my gosh, he might be having a heart attack." Man, I wish I could see her face. I bet it's more drained than mine.

Within a matter of seconds, a soft, fractured voice drifted towards my ears. "Matt! What's wrong? Can I do anything for you? Do you want me to find a paramedic?"

Even though my head was almost grazing the floor, I somehow managed to mumble, "No! Just woozy. Came on fast."

"Well, it's perfectly understandable. You haven't had any liquids since we've arrived, and you probably skipped breakfast, too. Am I right?" I moved my head up and down in slow motion like a turtle. "Add to that mixture the extremely hot weather, and you're just asking for trouble." I didn't respond. "Come on, Matt, lean on me, and I'll take you outside to get some fresh air."

"That might do the trick," I replied softly as I finally began a slow ascent. Although, I really felt the strange scenario my body just displayed was a simple case of premonitions. When I finally returned to my normal military stance, I searched the counter for the book I'd intended to purchase. It was gone. The clerk must've thought it was a no sale and put it away.

"I bet I know what you're looking for," Rita said, as she displayed the book resting in her hand.

"Yup. That's it. Thanks." I shoved my hand in my back pocket to retrieve my wallet.

"Put that away," my girlfriend commanded. "I paid for your book while you were examining the floor." She grabbed my free hand and quickly ushered me to the door. "Let's get out of here."

Why the hasty retreat, I silently wondered. Yes, I was still a little weak in the knees, but my embarrassing posture was resolved, and Rita's face certainly didn't display any telltale signs of ever having glowed like a beet. Could something else possibly be bugging her that I wasn't aware of? Shortly after the screen door slammed behind us, I went into investigative mode. "Okay, what was that fast departure all about?"

Rita batted her beautiful thick eyelashes a couple times before she innocently replied, "I was worried about you. That's all."

"No, there's more to it than that. What gives?"

"All right, all right, Mr. PI." She let loose of my arm. "Remember the guy who was waiting for the go ahead to start his machinery after the groundbreaking ceremony?"

"Ah … vaguely. The real sweaty guy sitting up in the Cat tractor, Ron?"

"Yes, he's the one."

"What about him?" I nonchalantly asked, worried that Rita had somehow become involved with him behind my back and now feeling guilty felt it was time for her to come clean.

No snap response materialized. Wow, things must be a lot worse than I'd feared. "I … Ah … don't know how to say this, Matt." I knew it. Here it comes, I thought. "Ron just wouldn't leave me alone." Oh, man! What did he do—call her non-stop or send her tons and tons of roses? I'm such a jerk. Why do I give Rita so much space? "Now, sweetie, I don't want you blaming yourself for what happened," she continued. Who the heck else should I blame? I should've given her an engagement ring a long time ago. I'm such a schmuck. "Now honey, I know you say you have premonitions, but that doesn't mean you can pick up on everything." Well, of course not, I thought to myself. I've never said I could. Even so, you'd think I would've picked up on this when it pertains to another man's having an interest in my girlfriend. "There's no way you could've possibly known that a man would make a pass at me in the history store."

"What?" She was being hit on—not wooed away from me. As anger hit me like a shotgun, my protective nature kicked into high gear. "So why didn't you tell me as soon as it happened?" I balled my hands into fists. "I would've loved to have shown him what my hands can do."

Rita stared at me. Her forehead was crinkled from her hairline to her nose. "How could I? There wasn't enough time—you bent over—he walked out."

I was so disgusted with myself. How could I not be there for Rita? A guy's supposed to watch out for his gal—that's engraved in stone somewhere. I stepped closer to Rita and gently wrapped my arm around her shoulders. "Babe, I'm so sorry you had to fend the idiot off by yourself, but I'm glued to your side now. I swear."

"Believe me, I'm holding you to that, mister," she said while she playfully jabbed her finger in front of my nose. "I guess what galls me the most is that the guy's married—pretty obvious—the white circle on his ring finger." She flung her arms out in front of herself. "Well, enough about him. Your queasiness wasn't actually heat related, was it?" I shook my head no. "I didn't think so. One of those premonition attacks, huh?"

I leaned my head towards hers ever so slightly, and then in a low tone of voice intended for her ears only, I honestly replied, "Yup, I'm fairly certain." I shoved the newly purchased book in front of her. "I think this triggered it; probably something to do with a future case."

Rita kept quiet. I suppose she didn't dare come up with another explanation since I've told her at least a dozen times that my premonitions aren't a bunch of malarkey. They actually help me solve cases. Of course, being a woman it's only natural to be suspicious of things she can't explain.

Comfortably positioning my girlfriend's soft warm hands between mine now, I decided it was time to interrupt whatever thoughts were still floating around in her intriguing head. "Hey, how do you feel about leaving our store adventures behind? I'd really like to resume the fun I was having earlier with this fantastic woman I know."

Her response to my question was a quick peck on the cheek.

Hmm ... nice, I thought to myself as I touched the damp spot on my face. I should say stuff like that more often. "Yum. Can I get a repeat performance?"

She wistfully whispered, "Later, but only if you behave yourself."

"Does that mean I have to let go of your hands?"

"I should say not," and she gripped my hands tighter.

"So what about the trolley ride? Do we want to do it or not?"

Rita returned to her well-known business tone now. "Well, according to this schedule, the next trolley tour isn't for a half-hour. So I guess our tennis shoes will have to take us where we want to go for roughly another thirty minutes. You don't really mind, do you? I mean, you're always bragging about the number of miles you and Gracie cover in a week."

"That's right," I answered sheepishly. Darn! Why do I brag to the extreme about the mutt's and my meanderings without sharing the part about being exhausted. I decided to add a silent contrition to my thoughts—forgive me— *Mea Culpa! Mea Culpa!*

While I withdrew inwardly for a moment, Rita pulled a folded pamphlet from her jacket pocket. "Here, Matt, you select the activities that you think I'd enjoy seeing. You're the one who has attended things like this before."

"Okay." I took the triple-folded program from her hand and scanned it. "Let's see, there's a late 1800's dance demonstration and an Indian Folk Lore presentation done to dance and song—by North Dakota Indians ..." At that exact moment a strange sensation engulfed me, but of course I ignored it. "There's also a skit entitled, 'Classroom Tales from 150 Years Ago'." The familiar school word automatically jangled bells in my head. "Classroom? Say, Rita, has your Uncle Harold spoken with you lately about the new middle school?"

"Yes, as a matter of fact he did, a couple days ago. It seems the excavation is humming along nicely."

"Good. I'm sure he's pleased that it's running so smoothly right now, but the next time you talk to him, remind him not to get too riled up when a construction problem arises; whenever that many people are involved in an extremely large project, it's only natural to run into a snag or two."

# CHAPTER 10

▼

**Mid-October**

I was being congratulated for winning the Grand Prix when a strange beast with fang-like claws entered the Winner Circle and pounced on the toes of my shoes tearing through leather and skin. I tried to shake the animal loose, but its nails were too deeply imbedded. Profanity followed profanity. Then I screamed, "Get off! Get off!" The shouting brought me to a semi-conscious state for only an instant, but it was enough time to make me wonder if I was really awake or dreaming. Sleepy as I was, I opted to bypass reality fairly quickly. I reached out for the wool blanket and tugged it closer to my unshaven chin, and then tried to return to the action in my unconscious world: the beast and his destruction of my time in the limelight.

It was useless. As hard as I tried, I just couldn't seem to get back to where I left off, even by flipping this way and that on the mattress. Disappointed, I slowly pried my eyelids open and took in the darkness of the evening. Shi ...! The ugly beast I'd been searching for was right here in my very own bedroom, standing at the foot of the bed smelling my feet which happened to be exposed to the elements. "So," I remarked, "you're up to your old tricks again. Well, I refuse to get up." For good measure I gruffly added, "Lay down, dog! Now!"

"Wuff-wuff. Wuff-wuff."

"Hey!" The darn mutt wasn't taking my orders seriously, and I didn't have a clue why. True, she has her stubborn streaks, but all in all she usually minds me. Not wanting to give up yet on the concept of the master being in charge of the household, I hurriedly thrust my hand in the direction of the wall farthest from me, and in a what I felt was a much firmer tone, repeated, "Lay down," which translates to *no snacks later for you, dog.*

"Wuff-wuff."

Dog-gone it! That tactic didn't work either. Shoot, now I have to get up. As I rolled my ample stomach from one side of the bed to the other, I asked myself why I was caving in. Wasn't I the king of this castle, the boss of this domain?

"Wuff-wuff."

Evidently not. "All right, all right, Gracie, you win." I wagged my index finger at her. "But I'm warning you, dog, your problem better be serious or you're in deep do-do trouble." Now I rubbed the gritty slumber from my eyes. The thought of leaving the warmth of the blanket behind didn't thrill me in the least, but I threw it off anyway.

This tiny action on my part really threw the dog's motivation into overdrive. She swiftly moved to the left side of the bed where I was sitting, displayed her teeth and clamped down on my unoccupied hand. If she was just an ounce stronger, she would have succeeded in dragging me off the bed.

I shook my head from side to side. At times like this, I wish the dog spoke human language. Then I wouldn't feel obligated to play charades with her. "Thirsty?" The mutt's mouth didn't move an inch, but a loud noise came from her just the same. Right after that, a different noise penetrated the room, a sound from outside the bedroom, a rapping. "Great! You've just managed to disturb our neighbors above and below us. Well, I'd better not get a warning from the apartment manager. Otherwise, we may find ourselves out in the cold." Gracie's tail wagged furiously. "Oh, yes, you may think that sounds lovely, but believe me you wouldn't like it."

She hastily released my hand and allowed one more "Wuff!" to escape.

"Shush!" I said as I leaned over and patted her head, hoping the touch of a hand might soothe her a little. It did.

The distant rapping came again, now, even though we were both as quiet as a cluster of grapes waiting to be eaten. This time, the pounding was quite a bit louder and was accompanied by a elderly female voice. "Matt, are you there?"

The dog recognized the voice sooner than I. She flew straight to the entrance door and began speaking to the invisible person. "Arf! Arf!"

A moment of silence followed on both sides of the door, and then the human voice commanded the dog to do something. "Gracie, go wake your master. Hurry!"

Remember how the dog didn't obey me earlier? Well, she sure listened to this order. She came buzzing back to the bedroom so fast it was like someone shot her out of a cannon. Of course, I was already standing in the doorway by this time and hastily moved. Otherwise the mutt would've knocked me flat for sure. Standing smack in front of me now, she barked wildly.

"Quiet! I understand." I yanked my hand away from her mouth before she could clamp down on it again and hollered at my late evening visitor, "Be there in a minute." I quickly finished covering my bottom half with sweat pants and took off across the long expanse of Berber carpet, with Gracie lagging only two steps behind. Reaching the door in record time, now, I popped the lock and security chain and then opened the door. "Why, Margaret, what a pleasant surprise. Come in."

My neighbor stared at me for a split-second before stepping into my abode. "Oh, dear, I"ve really caught you at a bad time, haven't I?"

Yes, you did, I wanted to reply. After all I was standing there disheveled from head to toe. But I couldn't move myself to do it. See, being what I think I am, basically a nice guy, I didn't want Margaret to feel bad so I lied. "Of course not. I was just catching a few z's on the sly before going to bed for the night. Isn't that what everybody does?"

I think she missed my answer completely because she apologized one more time. "Well, I'm really sorry I woke you, Matt, but I think you'll be pleased that I'm sharing my news with you tonight instead of waiting till morning."

At the mention of *news* my eyelids jarred to attention, and I swiftly absorbed the total Italian package standing in my midst: black pumps on her tiny feet and her favorite rose-colored dress coat. What type of news would bring her to my door at this late hour, my sensible deductive reasoning wanted to know. Perhaps she took a senior outing to a casino and hit it big.

Now I raised my hand and directed the same finger at my neighbor that I earlier used for the dog. "Oh, I understand now. You were out on the town tonight and you wanted to tell me all about it, right?" Margaret's lips remained tightly sealed as she slipped into one of my shabby chic chairs and got cozy. Need to put more fire on the fuel, Matt. "Ah, you and a male companion played the nickel slot machines at Mystic Lake Casino and hit the jackpot?" Her mouth barely loosened a fraction. She was making this guessing game extremely hard. I covered a yawn with the back of my hand now, and then I placed the same hand in front of her and said, "Wait ... don't answer, yet. You were with Tom, that fellow from Church?" I had forgotten his last name.

While my neighbor giggled, her face was transformed from a sallow complexion to a bright shade of pink. At least this game of mine was putting some fun into her life, I thought. "Stop teasing me, Matt. You know perfectly well I don't date Tom Campbell, and you are way off on your guessing. Tonight, I was a dinner guest of Evan and Claire Cox," she modestly reported. "Care to guess who was there, Mr. PI, besides me?"

"You know," I replied, "as much as I hate to say this, I haven't the foggiest notion. Just clue me in."

Reluctantly, my guest furnished the answer, "Rita's uncle—Harold Sinclair."

"Oh, really? Why was he invited to their house?"

"Because the worker who was excavating Evan's land unearthed a skull."

"A skull?? Did he dig up other bones with that?"

"No," Margaret softly responded, "just a skull. Apparently, the head of the construction crew notified the board as soon as it was found. They in turn called Evan. He seemed to think the skull could belong to one of his ancestors since a few were buried on the property."

I yawned again. "A, huh. Go on."

"Well, after we finished dinner it was still fairly early, so Evan suggested that each of us tackle one of his ancestral diaries in search of an answer."

"Hmm, interesting. Did anyone discover anything?" I sleepily quizzed.

As I stood there waiting for a response, I noted that the late night hour was taking its toll on my neighbor, too. Her hand rapidly moved to her mouth to stifle a yawn. "Sorry, I didn't realize how tired I was," she admitted.

"Perhaps a glass of water would help," I offered.

"Yes, that might do the trick."

I went to the kitchen, fetched a plastic glass from the cupboard, filled it with water, and returned to the living room where I presented the glass to my neighbor.

She took the glass from me. "Thank you." After a few sips were taken she then continued. "No, we didn't find anything of significance. All the ancestors mentioned in the diaries were dutifully buried in an old church cemetery somewhere in Anoka. Of course, we all agreed that a few deaths could have gone unrecorded depending on the circumstances."

I pondered Margaret's last statement before I replied. "I assume the police will be notified now."

My neighbor tried to focus her weary eyes on me. "Not necessarily."

"What do you mean?"

"If the police get dragged into this mess, the new school could be placed on the back burner indefinitely." That's true, I thought. "And you know how everyone involved in the building process has stressed the importance of opening the school on time." Her mouth shaped up for a yawn, but it was quickly diffused. "That's why I suggested you be given a crack at this skull dilemma."

My head snapped up hard like it did when I was in the Air Force. "Margaret, dear, even though I deeply appreciate your thoughtfulness, the police need to be notified. Have you forgotten that I almost got tossed in the slammer when Neil Welch didn't inform the St. Cloud Police about the break-in at his factory? Nope!" I said, "I'm not making enemies with any police department, not when I depend on their cooperation to solve cases."

As old as Mrs. Grimshaw is she didn't allow even a little sleepiness to dull her brain.

"Well, offer your assistance to the police then," she suggested. "You know how swamped they are with work. Why, I bet they'd appreciate the help. Besides, what harm can there be to look into the matter?" I had no idea, but I also didn't want to find out. She snapped her fingers. "If there's no missing person report on file that fits the description of the skull, it will simply be labeled and set on a shelf in some dark dank police department closet to become just another forgotten dust collecting object." Whoa Nellie. She spends way too much time watching crime shows, I thought to myself. She crossed her arms and tapped her size-five shoe on my carpet. "Matt, I know you too well. You're too nice a guy to condemn somebody's parents or siblings to a life of wondering what happened to their missing loved one. Come on, say it, you like helping the underdog."

"I do," I admitted under my breath. And she's right, the police were swamped with work, especially with the recent layoffs. But that didn't mean she had to pile a heavy guilt trip on me. After a few more minutes of meaningful mental prodding, I finally replied rather apprehensively, "Ah ... well, maybe I could look into this skull thing." Noticing that Margaret's eyes were opening and closing with even greater repetition now, I rushed to complete our late evening discussion.

"Should I call Mr. Cox in the morning, or will he be contacting me?"

She finally let a long-winded yawn escape. "Neither. Evan said to tell you that you're hired."

"Why, you sly fox, you."

"Seems to me someone used that line on me a time or two before," Margaret muttered, as she bent over, "but for the life of me, I can't remember who." Now she picked up a small floral gift bag resting by her feet and handed it to me. "Umm ... I almost forgot. This package is for you, but whatever you do," she warned, "don't drop it. The object is old and very fragile."

Why was she giving me a gift, I wondered. My birthday wasn't for several months yet. I accepted the bag and opened it in slow motion—the skull. "I must say Mr. Cox certainly has a unique way of hiring a PI." Normally, I meet with a client first and then go forward from there. That old saying, *beggars can't be choosers,* fits me perfectly. The way things had been going for me I didn't have the pleasure of being choosy. Finished with our little meeting now, I promptly ushered Margaret to the door. "Thanks for the present and the job," I said as I leaned on the door. "I really appreciate it."

"You're welcome," she replied as she pointed her short slim feet in the direction of her apartment, "And, the luck of the Irish to you."

Oops. I suddenly realized I had forgotten to ask my neighbor something of significance. I hurriedly poked my head out the door, hoping to catch her. "Ah, who do I report to, Evan Cox or Harold Sinclair?"

Margaret pulled her key from her lock, turned her body slightly towards me and replied, "Why, Harold Sinclair of course, but do bill Evan Cox." With that said, she slipped inside her apartment.

# CHAPTER 11

▼

Six A.M. came early. I was anxious to begin the task of jotting down notes about a case I was working on. Dressed only in boxer shorts and a v-neck undershirt I quickly plopped my body in front of the old battered mahogany desk residing in my tiny bedroom,. Paper and pen were already waiting so it was only a matter of putting the pen to work. My writing hand wasn't ready, however. It was too busy massaging my forehead. No, the Malone family didn't suffer from migraines, just sinus problems. Unfortunately, the mini-massage I was giving myself didn't seem to release any pressure. Well, I suppose my partial functioning brain can mull the case over instead.

"Mr. Harper, Mr. Harper," I chanted softly. "Where the heck are you hiding, and why can't I find a smidgen of information on you?"

The dog's ears jerked up when she heard my off-key voice. I think she assumed I was talking to her because she immediately jumped off the bed and made a hasty retreat to the other side of the room where she cast her head down like she does when she's been found guilty of a minor infraction. Poor dog.

"Sorry," I apologized. "I wasn't bawling you out." My left hand swiftly went for the wallet-sized photo of a very young Mr. Harper that Mrs Harper had given me. Now I stared at it intently. "You're probably sitting in some stinky bar right now laughing your fool head off, thinking you've outfoxed your wife. But have you really? You can only fly beneath the radar system for only so long, buddy, so watch out. This PI will be riding your tail real soon."

After rubbing my head another five minutes with nothing happening, I moved to the kitchen to prepare breakfast—coffee, orange juice, toast, and a bowl of *el cheapo* cereal. I know, you're probably wondering how I could think about eating when my head feels like it's about to drop off. The answer is simple. I figured maybe the old cold remedy that recommends feeding the cold and starving the fever, might just work for sinus problems, too. I dropped a thin slice of wheat bread in the toaster, and then I changed the dog's water, got a few doggie treats out, and managed to jam a couple spoonfuls of crunchy cereal into my mouth.

While I munched away, I thought about the skull presented to me in a bag last night. The case shouldn't be too tough to crack, but it demanded more legwork than normal. The easiest route to start the ball rolling would be by throwing a few "feelers" to the local police. Over the years I'd become quite chummy with a couple of the guys. Joe Murchinak, for instance, would be more than willing to give me an up-to-date report on Minnesota's Missing Persons.

From the size of the skull, I knew I could scratch a child's name off the list and any adult female too. Although, these days it's hard to know if a name is male or female. I'll definitely need to verify the sex on weird names. I had already guessed the top of the skull, the forehead, to be about a 7 ¾ hat size. Of course I could be wrong. I don't have a proper hat lying around in my abode to help me out. Every cap or hat I own simply says one size fits all. Same as all the tee shirts they sell now-a-days. So unless I was to meander into a hat department in a store such as Macy's or Herberger's and make an actual purchase, my guess-timate would have to stand.

My toast finally popped up. I quickly smothered it with gobs of peanut butter and strawberry jam and then took a bite. I suppose if my visit to the police station proves fruitless, I should drive over to St. Paul and check out the Science Museum. That place has got to have at least one room reserved in regards to human body parts. Darn! A tiny clump of peanut butter didn't want to leave the roof of my mouth so I stupidly took a gulp of scalding hot java. The peanut butter vanished but so did the roof of my mouth. "Whew!"

I picked up the breakfast dishes and carted them over to the sink where they could join the others abandoned the previous day. Then I escaped to the bedroom with Gracie clinging to my heels begging for attention.

"Not right now, girl, I'm busy." She whimpered for a bit, but then she gave up and crawled under my bed. As soon as the dog was hidden under the bed, an idea flashed across my brain cells. I wonder if it would be worth having a sketch drawn up of what the owner of the skull may have looked like. The latest technique to do such a thing is called computer morphing. The problem is it doesn't come free for me, and anyway, for all I know, the skull could still end up being a long deceased relative of Evan Cox.

The alarm clock on the night stand suddenly went off. It was eight-thirty and time to leave the apartment. I hopped on the elevator to ride to the basement garage where my filthy white Topaz resides. As usual, the floor of the car was looking a lot like the inside of a trash dumpster. The mess will need to be cleaned up one of these days but probably not until another date is set with Rita.

There wasn't much room to parallel park along the vertical stretch of road that ran in front of the police sub-station. Besides that, Hennepin Avenue is such a heavily traveled stretch of road that maneuvering the car in any direction is a dangerous game. After I finally managed to squeeze the car between two monstrosities, I got out and walked the few short steps to my destination. The sub-station I was about to enter was just one of many now existing in heavier crime related areas of town. So far the concept seemed to be working. Passing through the two sets of double glass doors, I studied the faces to see if I recognized anyone.

Ah, Sergeant Murchinak was at his desk, but his back was turned towards me. It appeared that he was preoccupied with the goings on outside his window as well as on his phone. Luckily, a fellow police officer seated next to him noticed me. He tapped Murchinak on the shoulder and pointed in my direction.

Murchinak quickly ended his conversation, stood, and strolled towards me. I evaluated the veins running along the front of his neck while waiting for him to reach me. They seemed to be considerably thicker today.

"Hey, Malone, what brings you here," Murchinak asked as he squeezed what little life I had in my hand, "early trick or treating?"

I laughed. "Something like that."

"Well, whatever your reason for being here, I just hope you haven't forgotten that when you show up this early in the morning you're expected to invite me to breakfast afterwards."

"Geez, is that all you cops think about is—food, food, food? The way you talk you'd think you were never allowed to escape for a snack. Why, it seems to me I read somewhere that precinct rules allow you guys to leave the premises for one quick meal a day."

The sergeant chuckled deeply. "Only if we're not behaving badly. But hey, at least it ain't a crime to think about food yet"

"Thank God," I swiftly replied as I rubbed my chubby stomach.

"So, you still solving all those crimes we cops don't have time for?"

"Of course." Okay, that's enough bantering, I thought to myself. Time to cut to the chase. "Hey, could you spare a few minutes of your time? I have a missing person situation I'm working on, and I could use your assistance."

"Sure, I can fit you in, Matt," he replied as he swung his right arm towards his desk where two huge stacks of paperwork waited for him. "As you can plainly see, there's no work on my desk requiring immediate attention." He quickly pointed to a chair in the corner of his office, "Oh, and look, the seat reserved for my *special guests* seems to be empty. Come on, drag it over here and start bending my ear."

I happily responded to Murchinak's command and began weaving my tale as soon as my butt grazed the chair, but the word skull never slipped through my lips, not once.

# CHAPTER 12

▼

Loosely cradling the current list of Minnesota's missing in my right hand now, I wandered effortlessly through the police sub-station's maze, anxious to get back to the Topaz and be on my way.

The police building had offered me refuge from the fresh fall air, but once outside the brutal wind smacked me hard in the face. I smartened up real fast though. I turned and offered my back to it and then continued on my way.

Well, ain't that grand. While I was gathering info, a nice collection of orange-hued leaves had collected on my car's windshield. I marched over to the window and flicked off as much as I could. Then I unlocked the door, dropped my overweight body on the Topaz's cold leather interior, and revved up the engine. Next destination, a hole-in-the-wall building located off Highway 65 and Lowry Avenue, better known as my office. I kinda figured since I was out and about, anyway, I should stop by the place and see what was cooking. In my line of business, one always holds out hope that there's a new client out there somewhere desperately trying to make contact.

Even though the building I do my business in isn't the Taj Mahal, it's still nice to know I can park wherever I want, since I'm the only tenant. Today, I situated the front of the Topaz so that it was directly lined up with the only entrance to the building. Right before I hopped out of the car, I followed my usual routine, scanning the surrounding area to make sure no one had tried to break in within the last couple of days. Nope, nothing seemed to be disturbed. I missed the mailperson, again though; various letters were crammed in the decrepit door's narrow rusty mail slot.

As much time as I take to analyze it, I'm still clueless as to why the mail delivery person bothers to force the mail through its designated opening when it's so much simpler to remove the bolts from the door's hinges and throw the mail in that way. Plus, I wouldn't have to get all sweaty from fighting with the mail everyday. I gripped the mail tightly and jumped backwards a few feet. That's the only way I know of to retrieve the items. Done! Now I tucked the mail under my arm, unlocked the door, and walked in.

I quickly tossed the mail on the mammoth desk where it could join the barely noticeable phone and all the other clutter. Whoa! What's that? The answer machine was trying to play "winkum and blinkum" with me, an old game teenagers used to play at house parties. I applied pressure to the play button with my thumb. Rita, my girlfriend, spoke first. She was wondering if I was free this weekend. She had something in mind. Could I please get back to her as soon as possible. I wasn't supposed to feel bad if I wasn't available; she'd just hook up with a girlfriend instead. The second caller wanted me to know about a carpet cleaning special that his company was running for small businesses this month. I could have three rooms cleaned for only seventy-five dollars. Who's he kidding? All my rental space comes with is a 10' x 12' loose piece of ugly orange shag carpet. Oh, the carpet tries to serve a purpose by pretending that the cracked cement floor slab beneath it doesn't exist. My mother left the final call. She said I hadn't called her in a couple days, and she wanted to make sure I wasn't lying dead somewhere. Why is it certain people know exactly which buttons to push to get a response out of you? All right, Mom, you win. I'll buzz you tonight.

Hmm ... as per the norm, nothing of significance was happening in my little corner of the world this morning. That means I could take off for St. Paul and no one would care. I hastily shoved my sleeve up so I could see the time on my watch: nine forty-five. Perfect timing. I'd arrive at the Science Museum just as the doors opened to the public.

# CHAPTER 13

▼

The lobby of the Science Museum was a disaster-waiting-to-happen—busloads of school-aged kids were swarming every which way. Darn! I didn't anticipate children running amuck. I've got important research to do. I rested my hands on my hips briefly and squeezed hard. Why the heck were the little ones running around? It's a school day; field trips usually take place in the spring when school's almost out and there's nothing more to do in the classroom. I eye-balled the tightly-filled lobby one more time hoping they'd disappeared. Unfortunately, nothing changed. Relax, Malone, I told myself. The small fry don't have to dampen your day. Just think of them as revolving doors—suck in your stomach and push on through.

I quickly dropped my hands to my side, inhaled deeply and then trudged forward towards the information window, all the while pretending the kids were invisible. It worked. The poor darlings didn't have a clue that an adult managed to cut in front of them. Now at the front of the line, I permitted my stomach to return to normal as I inquired about displays pertaining to the human anatomy. The very polite well-dressed elderly gentleman behind the counter informed me that if I went to the second floor I'd find what I was looking for.

I could've ridden an elevator to reach the second floor, there were four of them, but I opted for the stairwell instead. My legs needed the exercise. According to the volunteer I spoke with on the main floor, the third room on the right held what I was looking for, bones belonging to the human body.

I was at the second floor landing so I opened the door and walked briskly down the narrow hallway, counting the room openings as I went along. As per the norm, information regarding each display was posted outside the rooms.

When I finally reached the third room, I stopped and read the plaque posted alongside the doorway. Skulls were at the back of the room. Knowing where to proceed to now, my eyes quickly shifted from the plaque to the inside of the room. It was at this juncture that I hit a bit of a snag. You see, fifth graders were doing a fine job of hiding the display with their line-dance routine. Hmm ... what to do, what to do.

As I stood in the doorway killing time, thoughts of long-ago field trips raced through my old memory bank. Boy, those teachers sure kept us on a tight schedule. We weren't allowed to dilly dally for nothing. Every minute counted. As a matter of fact when I was in second grade, a classmate of mine, Billy White, almost got left at Como Zoo. A child's sneeze finally busted up my memories of long ago, and I once again realized where I was and what I was up to. I ran a hand through my hair and then moved to the bone displays in the center aisle. I know I didn't come to study body bones, but I figured as long as I couldn't get at the skull display, for the time being, I might as well as absorb some other scientific information.

Ten minutes later the tour guide cleared her throat and said, "All right, boys and girls, please line up quickly. The movie in the Omni Theater will be starting shortly, and we mustn't be late for the show."

Yes, children, I said internally, please don't dawdle. I'd like to study a certain display that you have been blocking for far too long. Two lines instantly formed. It was as if my thoughts were transferred to the kids, but I knew that wasn't possible. A second later, the group dispersed.

Before saddling up to my destination, I whipped out a notepad and pen for recording helpful information. Ahh, such nice kids! The glass display case, which I'm sure was squeaky clean earlier this morning, was smudged from one end to the other; all thirty fifth-graders had left their fingerprints behind for prosperity. Luckily there was a solution to the problem. I turned my shirt sleeve into an eraser and removed most of the smudges. There. Much better.

The case contained a sufficient amount of skulls for studying purposes, ranging in sizes from infant to mature adult, but since I was only concerned with adult skulls, I wouldn't waste precious time reading the note cards displayed with the younger-aged skulls. Before I could begin studying any notes, however, my eyes required the assistance of reading glasses. Luckily, they were in one of my shirt pockets so I retrieved them and perched them on the edge of my nose. With that out of the way now, I finally lowered the upper portion of my body.

In this position, the bulging part of my stomach touched the case, but I didn't care. It wouldn't smudge the glass. Hmm, I still couldn't read the cards. Either I was ready for an eye exam, or the writing was much smaller than the majority of eyes could handle. I fidgeted with the specs for a sec hoping it resolved the problem, and then I positioned them on my nose again. Ready to re-read the cards, I leaned even closer to the case than before. That's when a loud beeping sound began emanating from somewhere. Crap, I must've set off a darn alarm, I thought.

Hmm … I wonder how long I have before someone comes to see what's going on. I decided to take a chance and look under the case before I was escorted out. "Nuts! There's nothing there!" I whispered to the air. And the beeping continued. Confused, I dropped my hands and let them rest next to my pant pockets. "Ah, crap!" My new pager was the culprit.

Today was the first day I was carrying it since receiving the gizmo for my birthday a few months before. I never wanted one of these fool things, but my parents thought otherwise. When I opened my gift, my mother said, "Can't have you living in the dark ages son, you being a PI. Dad and I discussed what you could use for your line of work, and well, we decided this would be perfect. Now, Matt, make sure you use it. Promise us you won't throw it in the back of your sock drawer like you did with the all toys you didn't like when you were little." And of course, that's exactly what I did. I tossed it in the back of the sock drawer and didn't discover it until yesterday when I was in dire need of a certain colored sock.

Since I hadn't given out my pager number to my clients yet, it was obvious that a family member was trying to reach me. I felt my pockets for the cell phone. Dang it! I'd left it at the office. I raced out of the skull area as fast as my legs permitted in search of a tour guide. Finally finding a woman guide at the other end of the hallway of the floor I was on, I swiftly inquired about the nearest pay phone. "One floor down and next to the bathrooms," came her crisp reply.

Sweat was rolling profusely off my hands as my fingers danced to the button tones. Mom answered on the first ring. Her usual cheery voice was replaced with a subdued tone in between bouts of crying. "An ambulance is supposed to be arriving any minute for your father. The doctor thinks he may be having a heart attack. Matt, tell me you can meet me at the hospital?"

"Yes!" I shouted into the phone as a think lump formed in my throat. "Where are they taking him?"

My mother's answer sounded forced, like she was trying to control her sobbing. "Ab … Abbott Northwestern."

I was in St. Paul, and the hospital was located in Minneapolis, but it wouldn't take me long to get there. I knew a back way. I was very thankful when my mom said that my father was being taken to Abbott Northwestern. It's one of Minnesota's top hospitals for heart care. Trying to control my emotions, I spoke in as calm a tone as I could handle. "I'm leaving right now. Wait for me in the emergency area." Uncontrollable sobbing hastily flowed through the phone lines to me, now, and I blended my crying to the mix. "Everything's going to be all right, you'll see." Then I whispered, "Love you, Mom."

Of course, everything wasn't all right as I soon learned. After Dad had a procedure called angioplasty, it was determined that he would need to have quadruple bypass surgery performed. "Too much rich food's the main culprit," the doctor said. "When I spoke with your father's personal physician earlier, he said he wasn't surprised that your father ended up here. He's been warning him about his high cholesterol for years."

I gave Mom an inquiring look, but she said nothing. No one ever mentioned that Dad had high cholesterol. Just blame it on another one of those things men don't talk about, I guess.

Once my other siblings arrived, we discussed the type of support system our mother might need during Dad's stay at the hospital. The final consensus was that we kids should take turns driving her to the hospital and staying with her. Of course, since I supposedly didn't have a *real* job, I landed the day shift which meant my science museum research was out of bounds for at least the next seven days.

The first day, after my father's non-complicated surgery, found me wandering the halls looking for a pay phone again. I needed to notify Harold Sinclair that I'd positively identified the skull Margaret had given me as human. At least I was able to determine that before I had to zip out of the museum. My cell phone was with me this time, not like the other day at the Science Museum, but the hospital asks that you don't use it on certain floors: safety reasons. I turned the corner—another hallway and still no phone. My handy dandy cell phone was really itching to be used. I'd better find a different phone soon. Now I took another hallway. While I'm at it, I should probably tell Harold my visit to a local police station was a complete washout; there were no men on the most recent list of missing persons, only women. "Ah, finally."

Harold picked up on the first ring and remained politely silent while I filled him in. When I was completely finished he only offered words of encouragement in regards to my dad's condition. I was extremely relieved and yet surprised that he hadn't mentioned the skull. Before calling him, I was certain our conversation would end with me being pressured into getting the skull situation resolved as quickly as possible, especially since he made no secret of his strong feelings pertaining to school construction delays.

"Thanks for the kind words, Harold. I'll definitely pass them on to my family." I twisted the band of my watch a little, so I could see the time. "Oh, crap!" I didn't realize I'd left my mother alone for so long. "Harold, I gotta get back to the cardiac floor pronto, but as soon as I can sneak away to do more research, I'll give you a jingle."

"Matt!"

"Yeah?"

"Our research can wait, but your family can't."

# CHAPTER 14

▼

**End of October**

Since Dad showed no signs of complications from his heart surgery the week before, one of the nurses on the cardiac care floor said he would probably be released in a day or two. Heck, that meant Dad's doctor could be making the big announcement right now, as I zipped down the highway with Mom at my side heading for Abbott Northwestern Hospital.

For the last fifteen minutes or so of our journey, Mom had sat tight-lipped while the cars in the faster lanes had buzzed by us, but now as we approached the hospital, she finally thawed and shared her thoughts on how she planned to handle things once Dad rejoined her. I tried to ask her how I might help, but she didn't give me the chance. She just patted my right leg and said, "Now, Matt, I don't want you or your brother to be concerned about the fall chores. Things are in good shape. Why, last month your father washed the windows, covered my perennials with mulch, and raked the leaves. It was almost as if he knew that would be his only chance to do it," then she sighed. "I just don't know what I'm going to do during the snowy season. I can't shovel because of my back, and I'm forever fretting about having an accident when I need to drive somewhere."

"Not a problem," I said as I pulled into the hospital's huge parking lot, "Your kids, including myself, can help shovel and take turns running errands for you when winter arrives."

When we neared my Dad's room, the head nurse stopped us. "Hi," she said in a very pleasant tone. "I thought you'd like to know that Mr. Malone hasn't been visited by his doctor yet because he was called into emergency surgery." She glanced down at the silver watch on her left wrist, said, "It'll probably be eleven or a little later before he gets to his rounds," then she vanished back to her station.

Well, to be accurate, the middle-aged doctor finally showed his face closer to noon. "Hi, how's everyone doing?" he asked when he walked in. "I'm not interrupting anything, am I?"

Dad managed to sit up as straight as he could in the hospital bed before replying. "No, not at all. We were just discussing the possibility of my leaving here today. So what's the verdict going to be, doc?"

The doctor didn't reply until he performed a routine examination of Dad. "Everything's looking good, Mr. Malone. I don't see why you can't go home within the next hour if you promise me that you'll adhere to the strict diet and exercise regime we've planned out for you."

It was now past noon, and my father's stomach was growling. He swiftly raised his right hand and swore he'd faithfully follow the health guidelines given to him a few days before. Half-hidden by my father's wheelchair, Mom and I tossed each other a knowing glance. Dad adhering to a plan? Come on. Well, maybe I was wrong. Perhaps this surgery was a big enough wake up call for him.

The minute our shoes hit the main floor of the hospital, my brother met us and took over the taxi service. Since his car was already parked along the curbing by the main entrance, I helped him get Dad into the car and said my good-byes. Now it was time to head to the Topaz where I had left it at nine this morning: the edge of the parking lot. Being an unusually cold October day, the car required a few minutes to warm up.

I purposely ignored news of any kind this past week, but now I felt it was my civic duty to tune in. Heck, I wouldn't be able to converse with the common man on the street if I didn't do so. I pushed the radio knob in and waited for the host of the hour. Not many people know this, but I really hate listening to the news—most of the information shared with the public makes me boil. But like I said, I need to be informed. KRRN was on the ball as usual. "The Dow went up sharply, but NASDAQ went way down." Stock traders' lingo. "The corn trade is low due to the better than expected weather conditions in China.... Rain is called for today. At present it is partly cloudy or partly sunny depending on your disposition. And in the local news—a human skull was uncovered in Oak Grove on the property that used to belong to Evan Cox."

"Holy Shi...." I shrieked.

Another radio voice jumped in, "Hey, isn't that where the new middle school is being built?"

"You're right, Bob," the news commentator replied. "Wow, that sounds like a Rip Van Winkle story to me. Student falls into a deep sleep while waiting for school to be built. Several decades later, student awakes to find the school was never built. Alas, the shock is too much for the poor fellow; he drops dead on the spot." There's a tremendous amount of laughter going on at the station. "Oops, sorry folks. That last comment was in poor taste. Please don't write or call the station. I was only joking."

"You may be kidding around," I said aloud, "but I want to know who's passing private information onto the press?" Time to make a phone call. My hands twisted the steering wheel sharply clockwise causing the car to lurch towards the right shoulder of the road. Crap! I gave too much spin to the wheel. I needed to do something right away or I'd end up in the ditch. I braked as hard as I could. There—that did it. I was still on solid ground.

Disgusted with what I'd just heard on the radio as well as my current driving technique, I roughly brushed the heel of my hand through my hair. "Damn! Evan Cox, Harold, and the other school board members are going to think I leaked the information." If there's one thing I can't stand it's clients thinking I'm a snitch. When I worked for Neil Welch, President of Delight Bottling Company, he thought I had handed over some confidential information to select European newspapers. Of course, it was proven rather quickly that his assumption was wrong. But still, while it's being resolved everyone treats you like a bitter pill.

I removed a hand from the steering column so I could search the glove compartment for the cell phone. That's where I tossed it when I got in the car. The huge collection of straws and napkins, obtained from various fast food places over the years, was doing an excellent job of hiding it. "Ah, there you are." I pulled the phone out and shoved the other junk back where it came from, and then my fingers began poking at the buttons on the phone. "Hello, you have reached the residence of Mr. and Mrs. Harold Sinclair. We are not able to take your call, right now, but if you leave your name and number, we'll get back to you as soon as we can. Beep …"

Crap, I was hoping he'd be home. "Yeah, Harold, it's me, Matt Malone. Just heard the latest news broadcast. I see the press got wind of the skull find. My hunch is one of the construction guys loosened their lips at a local watering hole. If you want to talk, you know how to reach me." I turned the cell phone off and threw it on the seat next to me. "Okay," I mumbled, "might as well scratch the museum since the cat's out of the bag. But there must be something else I can do, right now. Evan hasn't cancelled my services yet." Let's see. I could drive out to the sight—see exactly where the skull was discovered. I rubbed my fingers back and forth across my head, as if that would help me come to some sort of conclusion. I guess the digging sight is where I shall roam.

Just as I was about to swing back onto the roadway, music from *Born in the U.S.A.* began playing. It was the cell phone. I reached over and picked it up. "Matt Malone, Private Investigator, how may I help you?"

"Mr. Malone. Thank God I found you," the highly emotional woman's voice blurted out. "I've got fantastic news."

"Wonderful! Care to fill me in, Mrs. Harper?"

"Of course. My missing man has been sighted in the Hinkley area."

"The Hinkley area? Really?"

Violet Harper screamed into the phone, "Spotted at the casino. Can you believe it? I knew he was spending all our hard earned money."

"Before we go any further," I said, "how reliable is your source, and when did they actually see your husband?"

"Close friends of mine saw him. We used to play cards together. Marsha and Stan said they saw him less than an hour ago."

My right ear was going numb. It was time to switch the phone to the other ear. "You realize he could be long gone by now, and I'd hate to have to charge you for nothing."

Mrs. Harper spoke with a more demanding voice now. "Look, Mr. Malone, I don 't care how much it costs to track that weasel down. You just find him."

"Okay, whatever you say, Mrs. Harper. I'll get right on it. By the way, did your friends happen to tell you what section of the casino they saw your husband in, or describe what he was wearing?" As I waited for her reply, I reached in the glove compartment again to retrieve a pen and notepad. "Ah, huh. Ah, Huh. Thanks. Like I said, I'll check it out and get back to you." I pressed the End button and placed the cell phone back on the passenger seat. "Shoot!" There goes my visit to the construction sight.

# CHAPTER 15

▼

**November**

Two weeks ago the airwaves blasted the skull info into every Minnesota home, but I still was waiting in limbo for the other shoe to drop, namely receiving a call from Harold saying my assistance was no longer required. I grabbed the daily newspaper off the kitchen table where I had been sitting, brought it into the livingroom, and sat down in my recliner with it. I really hate being left in the dark when I depend on every nickel I earn to pay the bills. Perhaps Rita's uncle was merely holding off on the bad news until he saw what the police came up with, now that the problem's in their ball court. Too bad I'm not acquainted with the investigating cops. Oh, well, if I don't hear from Harold by the time the questioning wanes, I guess I can step in and finish the job.

My eyes quickly scanned the front section of the paper looking for anything related to a skull. The smattering of articles I eventually found appeared redundant; Saint Francis police scoured every inch of school property looking for more clues—nothing's been uncovered—still bringing in people to be questioned.

What a mess! I tossed the paper on the carpet. My hands were temporarily tied in regards to the skull situation, and the husband in my only other case was still on the prowl. It was crazy to think he'd stick around the casino for any length of time; in a casino/hotel a person can easily vanish within a second or two of being seen. Darn! Looks like the Harper case could end up being one of those sit and wait deals, too.

Two cases in a holding pattern. What other option does that leave me with this morning? Hmm … spending time with the dog, which isn't too bad, except I'd much rather do something with my lovely lady, Rita. Unfortunately, I knew she wasn't available—up to her elbows in marketing work as usual.

And the dog wins. "Where are you, mutt?" I called out. "Time for a brisk walk around your favorite park." The word park drew Gracie out. She made a mad dash from the kitchen to the hallway. Apparently she had been hiding under the kitchen table all along. I grabbed her leash and hitched it to her collar. Then I hauled my lightweight winter boots out of the hall closet along with my new Columbia jacket, put them on, and we were on our way.

Since it was a down day for me, I decided that the dog and I didn't need to take the fastest route out of the Foley Complex, the elevator; we'd walk down the four flights of stairs instead. Besides, the steps would get my old heart pumping sooner.

The lobby was empty when we entered it which was what I was hoping for. I get tired of hearing people say, "Off today, Malone, huh?" The way they ask makes it sound like I only fool around when I'm in the building. Living in an apartment certainly has its downsides—running into a nosy person is just one of them.

As soon as we passed through the apartment's double entrance doors and the fresh crisp air greeted us, Gracie let me know she had something to do, and she was going to do it, no matter what, so I led her to the nearest fire hydrant as fast as I could and got out of her way.

When I was positive her mission was completed, I said, "Are you ready to head over to the park now?"

Being the smart dog I brag her up to be, she instantly replied, "Wuff, Wuff," and then tore off in the direction of Loring Park.

Crud! The benches surrounding the perimeter of the park were mounded with snow. That means the dog and I wouldn't be taking any breaks in between our jaunts. Oh, heck, I shouldn't be taking breaks anyway—I can't get my heart rate up if I'm forever resting.

Gracie and I had just rounded the park for the second time when my pager went off. That's the nice thing about living only a few blocks from the park. I can get back to the apartment in a flash if I need to. I stopped and inhaled deeply. I wasn't exactly eager to see the number of the caller since the last page I received, from my mother, had brought bad news. I blew out what I inhaled, sucked in more fresh air, then took the pager out of my coat pocket and stared at the number. It wasn't my mother, but it was bad news all the same. "The shoe's about to be dropped Gracie. Time to go home." The mutt tilted her head enough to allow her huge soulful eyes to eyeball me at just the right angle. "That's the way it is. I can't change it. If you want shelter and food, I have to work." I yanked on her leash a couple times until she finally gave in.

Back at my apartment, now, I dialed the number displayed on my pager and waited.

"Matt, thanks for returning my call so fast," Harold Sinclair said. "I was hoping you had your pager on."

I swiftly responded, "Well, I don't usually make it a habit to carry it when I'm running, but today my instincts told me to bring it along." I slipped my jacket off while bracing the earphone piece between my ear and my neck. "I suppose you're calling to tell me the police figured everything out?"

"That's correct. Once Mr. Cox was informed of the details, he asked me to thank you for your help and to say your services are no longer required."

*No longer required,* those three miserable words could disappear from the English language, and I wouldn't miss them in the least. Dang! Less money for paying bills. "Well, where did the skull come from?" I hastily asked as I kicked my boots off. "Was it part of Evan's past?"

Harold laughed. At least one of us was in a jovial mood. "No, no," he replied. "This wasn't from one of Evan's ancestors. It turns out one of the district's sixth grade science teachers planted it. The fella was supposed to transfer to the new school when it was ready. Doesn't look like he'll be doing that now. Too bad— he's one of the best science instructors we've got."

"Did he say why he did it?" I asked.

"Joking around, supposedly. Which is probably true since I heard he has quite a reputation as a prankster."

"Will he get canned?"

"Not for me to say," Harold replied cautiously, "but there comes a time when enough is enough."

"I hear you," I said. "It's too bad I didn't have time to figure out what was going on before the police got wind of it. Oh, well, thanks for filling me in, Harold."

"Don't give it a second thought, Matt. You had a lot on your plate in your personal life. Now listen, don't forget, you and Rita are supposed to come over for dinner some Sunday." Click.

# CHAPTER 16

▼

After I finished my short conversation with Harold Sinclair, I strolled over to the desk in my bedroom and flipped through the calendar—pretty wide open. Things were pretty bleak. No inkling where Harper was, and now the work for Mr. Cox had been cancelled. I needed to find more reliable work, pronto, or I'd be sitting in the dark soon without heat, something I couldn't afford to happen to me this time of year. Of course, my third cousin, Steve, said if I ever needed to pick up a few bucks, I could help out at his car wash on the other side of town. "Nah, no way." Something will fall in my lap before I have to revert to that. I bit my lower lip. At least, I hope so.

The dog meandered into the bedroom, in search of me I suppose, and jumped on the bed. "Sure, go ahead, be lazy," I said sarcastically. "You don't have to worry about a thing. You have such a rough life."

Gracie responded to my complaining with a "Ruff."

"Smart aleck. But hey, thanks for the brilliant idea you just gave me. I'm going to teach you all kinds of neat tricks so I can send you around the country to audition for plays and movies." I had just read in the paper that one guy's dog is in high demand for stage performances of *Wizard of Oz*. I rubbed my hands together. Yeah, having the dog work for money sounded darn good to me. "Our roles would be reversed, Gracie. Why, then I'd get to flop on the bed all day and depend on you for my food and housing. What do you think of that?"

The dog shoved her long narrow face into the blankets and covered her head with her paws. I think she was trying to tell me she had heard enough and she didn't appreciate where this conversation was going.

"Okay, okay. You're right. I'm the human here and the one who has to support us. But if you hear of any opportunities while you're gallivanting around town with your fellow friends, be sure to let me know, would you."

The morning was shot, and I couldn't think of anything to do at the moment except fix lunch. Whenever I'm worried about meeting my obligations, I stuff my face. That seems to work for a lot of people. Hmm ... a bowl of leftover chili would certainly clear my brain cells. I've actually had great revelations while eating some really hot versions. Obviously not often enough, though, or I wouldn't have so many money predicaments.

I didn't feel like washing a bunch of dishes later so I simply took the pot containing the chili out of the fridge, heated it, and ate right out of the pan. I was just swallowing the last spoonful when a thought crossed my mind. Maybe the only way I'm going to find Harper is if he tries to find a buyer for those heirloom silver candlesticks he swiped from his wife. Violet had given me an excellent description of them—they had been in her family since the 1800's. I had made up flyers and sent them off to antique stores and pawnshops in the surrounding suburbs quite a while ago, but as of yet I had not gotten any response.

Knock. Knock.

Who the heck was that, I wondered.

Gracie, who sometimes thought she was a watchdog, quickly bounded into the kitchen to make me aware of the situation. "I heard. Thank you for the notification though." I set the empty kettle in the sink and immediately went to the door. Since our landlord didn't provide us with peepholes, I've always left the chain on for safety measures and then only slightly cracked the door. And so that's what I did today. "Oh, hi, Margaret." I unhooked the chain and spread the door wide open. "Come on in."

The dog took full advantage of the situation and tried to sneak into the hallway before my female company could slip into the apartment. "No! Stay!" I ordered. Of course, the elderly visitor misinterpreted the command I had just given. She immediately stopped in her tracks and stared wide-eyed at me. "Sorry, Margaret, I didn't mean you. That order was for Gracie."

Luckily the mutt obeyed me too, and I quickly took hold of her collar to allow Margaret admittance. Once she crossed my threshold, I let go of Gracie, shut the door and then showed my neighbor to the couch. "It's been awhile since we've seen each other, hasn't it?" I said as I sat in my Lazy-Boy chair. "So, how have you been?"

Margaret fluffed her thin hair. "Me?" she replied in her soft voice. "Couldn't be better."

Oh, crap. I just realized I'd forgotten to call her back the other night. "Geez, I'm sorry I forgot to return your call. I had a lot on my mind." I ran my hand through my hair now.

"No need to apologize, Matt."

"Well, I did promise to give you the low down on my dad. The doctor says he's on the mend so I guess that's about all we can hope for."

She must've been in the middle of some baking project or something before crossing the hall because she was wearing her rose patterned apron which she patted with her hands now. "Good, I'm glad to hear that he's doing okay."

"So what brings you my way?"

"Well, I want to season meat for a casserole I'm preparing, but I can't seem to get the lid off the minced onion jar. These arthritic fingers of mine aren't cooperating," she said flashing her crippled fingers in front of me. Boy, how organized can one get—making supper in the morning. I on the other hand wait till the last minute to pull my surprise microwave supper from the freezer. She continued. "Could you come over and loosen the lid for me?"

"Oh, sure, just give me a second." I led Gracie to the kitchen, told her to stay, and then Margaret and I trotted off to her apartment.

\*         \*         \*         \*

When I returned home a half-hour later, I found the mutt sprawled out in my beefy-leather-recliner, snoring. So much for obeying her master. I tiptoed past her and quickly made my way to the nearest phone. I was curious to see if I'd missed any calls. Yup, there was one lone message waiting for me. I immediately replayed it.

"Yes," a male voice said in a hushed tone. "I'm calling about the flier you sent to our antique store. A person who works here is trying to sell a set of silver candlesticks exactly like the pair in the picture."

Time's up! I poked my finger into the empty air. "Got'cha, Harper."

The messenger's voice remained low in tone as he continued, "You can reach me at 763-441-2822. Make sure to ask for Don."

I hurriedly pressed the numbers and waited. "Hello, could I speak to Don, please?" There was a lot of static on the other end of the line, and then I heard someone fumble with the phone.

"This is Don," the elderly tenor voice said. "What can I do for you?"

"Don, this is Matt Malone. You just left a message about a pair of silver candlesticks," I said as I sat down on the edge of my bed and made myself comfortable.

"Oh, sure. Well, I thought you'd like to know as soon as possible."

"You bet. Thanks for taking the time to notify me. Will the person you mentioned in your message be there later this afternoon? I'd like to speak with him or her."

"Ah, just a minute. I need to take a look at the schedule. It's kept right here by the phone." I heard pages being turned, then the elderly gent was back on the line. "He comes in around three and works till six."

"Well, listen Don, if this connects to what I'm working on, I'll see that you get some sort of compensation. How does that sound?"

"Wonderful," Don said. "Being retired, I never turn down extra income."

"Glad to hear that. Now how about filling me in on this guy's looks." I'd be darned if I was going on another wild turkey hunt.

While I waited for Don's response, I heard coins being tossed into a container of some sort. "Sure," he finally replied. "Let's see ... He's six-feet tall, tan complexion, hasn't worked here long ..."

# CHAPTER 17

▼

Three-thirty. I entered the Foley's lackluster elevator and quickly pressed the button for the basement level, the apartment's underground parking area where the ever-faithful filthy Topaz sits usually hemmed in by two new off-the-showroom-floor Jeep Cherokees.

A minute later, the elevator door slid back and revealed exactly what I was expecting; the Topaz dwarfed by its two shiny companions. I strolled to the front of the car and patted its hood just before entering it; the car may be an inanimate object, but I still wanted to let it know I understood. Once that was finished, I opened the door on the driver's side, parked my butt on the front seat, revved up the engine, backed out of the stall, and then patiently waited to exit.

The Foley's mammoth garage door finally sensed that a car wanted to escape its clutches and opened its jaws. When enough clearance was available, I shot out of the labyrinth and swiftly hung a left which would get me over to Interstate 94 and eventually to all other roads leading into Elk River. The drive from downtown Minneapolis to Chubbs Antique store would take about twenty-five minutes.

Traffic heading north was heavy, but not as crammed as the last day of the work week. If it were Friday, instead of Wednesday, I'd be in bumper-to-bumper gridlock with those crazy city dwellers traveling north seeking outdoor fun. The town of Brainerd supposedly got four inches of new snow around two this morning.

The clock in the car said it was three-fifty when I passed the metal elk sculpture which denotes one's arrival to the Elk River area. Hmm, must've been going a wee bit over the speed limit to get here five minutes early. As I slowed the car down to thirty-miles per hour, I studied all the shop signs. Considering that the town of Elk River was classified as small, I'd say it had plenty to offer for citizens of the town as well as out-of-towners. The downtown area consisted of a few fast-food eateries, a couple banks, Murphy's corner drugstore, St. Isadora's Catholic Gift Shop, Mary Sue's Doll Repair, a craft store called Walt's, a stamping store, and Chubbs. There was even a free ground level parking lot provided by the merchants situated between Jackson Avenue and Highway 10. A very generous gift to the public. Now if only the downtown Minneapolis merchants would get off their duffs and offer free parking too.

I parked the Topaz so that the nicer end, the front, faced Highway 10, and then I shut the motor off and zipped up my jacket. Since I wasn't in any rush to scramble across the street, I allowed myself time to recall Don's words again in regards to Glen Wilson. He hadn't been in town long and no mention of family—red flag big time. And the piece de` re`sistance is the guy's in his mid-thirties and has the same height and hair coloring as my man on the lam. Well, in just a couple minutes, I'll know if Glen is truly Brad Harper or not. For Violet's sake, I hope I've hit the jackpot this time.

I wasn't the least bit concerned about Wilson figuring out what I was up to since I had concocted a believable enough story during the drive here. Why, I was merely a brother dashing around town hunting for an appropriate silver-wedding anniversary gift to give his sister and her hubby. Now I locked the car door and walked across the street to Chubbs.

A small bell jangled above my head when I pushed the door open. An older gentleman perched on a high stool behind a glass counter, which contained a few unique antiques, peered up from his magazine as I entered. In a melodramatic tone, I quietly inquired if he was Don. The seventy-something man, with graying thin hair around his temples and a mole on his forehead, nodded in the affirmative. I immediately whipped out my business card and slid it across the counter. He glanced at it for a fraction of a second, and then he picked it up and hurriedly stashed it in the pocket of his flannel shirt.

Okay, we've made our connection. Time to begin a conversation in a normal tone of voice, I thought. "Hi, I was wondering if you might have something for sale that would be appropriate to give for a twenty-fifth wedding anniversary?"

At first Don acted like he wasn't quite sure how to respond, but then he nodded his head and said, "Mister, you're in luck. It just so happens we carry a large amount of silver items, and that's generally what one gives for a twenty-fifth or Silver anniversary. We could narrow down your selection process though if you had an idea of what you might like to purchase. Perhaps a bowl, a fancy serving plate, cups, or possibly candlesticks?"

"Hmm, yeah, I think a set of candlesticks for their dining room table would be appropriate."

"Great choice," Don said as he rubbed his jagged jaw and started moving out from behind the counter. "I don't handle the sales for the silver items, but I'll get someone who's very knowledgeable about that stuff," and he tilted his head in the direction of the second floor. "Say, Glen, could you come down here? I have a customer who needs your assistance on the main floor."

The person known as Glen was half-hidden by the thick wooden rails surrounding the upper floor, so for now all I could do was listen for his reply. "Sure thing, Don. Be right there." The voice I heard was pleasant sounding, but it didn't really resolve anything since I was never given a tape with Brad Harper's voice on it.

Heavy footsteps clashed with the wooden stairs as they made their way to the main floor, and then he was there. "Hi, what can I help you with?"

The eyes and hair were wrong. Crap! Sorry Violet, this ain't your old man. Glen's eyes were blue—not brown, and his hair was curly not straight. Granted, those two things could very easily be altered, but a huge birthmark is a different story. Mr. Harper's dragon-shaped birthmark is located at the mid-section of his right arm; Don's new employee was wearing a short-sleeved shirt, and his skin was anything but marked. I was disappointed, of course, but I decided to play this charade through anyway, since I was fairly certain the candlesticks Don told me about belonged to Violet.

"Yes, I was just telling the other gentleman, Don, that I need a gift for my sister's twenty-fifth wedding anniversary. I'm thinking of purchasing a pair of silver candlesticks."

Mr. Wilson appeared to be more concerned about an object outside the antique store than with what I just said. What exactly was going through his mind, I wondered. "Ah, of course, we have plenty of silver candlesticks on hand. I'm sure you'll find just the right set for your sister and her husband." Oh, I know I will, I thought to myself. "You might want to consider whether age is important."

I tried to break the ice, "Only if we're not talking about me."

He didn't find my comment amusing. "Okay, just let me get some keys I'll need." He leaned his body across the front counter and grabbed a set of keys hanging on a hook. "Now, if you'll follow me to the room in the back, I'll show you what we have on hand."

Only a few steps were required to reach the back room. "These candlesticks you have for sale are in pretty good shape, aren't they?"

"Absolutely!" Glen stopped by the first display cabinet. "We don't sell silver items unless they are in excellent condition or close to it. See for yourself."

"Yes, you have a very nice assortment," I replied, "I'm impressed."

The man assisting me now placed a tiny key in the white cabinet door and opened it. Then he turned to me and asked, "Do you want your gift to be sterling silver or silver plated?"

"Hmm ... I guess I'd prefer sterling unless I see something in silver plated that appeals to me, like maybe that set over there." I pointed to the plain pair sitting in the display case next to the one he just opened; they were only six-inches high. The Harper's candle holders were the complete opposite: ornate and over a foot tall. "How old are those?"

"I'm afraid I'm not familiar with them—I've only worked here a short time. Let me take a quick look at the tag." Glen moved to the second case and immediately began shaking his head, "Someone forgot to flip the information card right side up." He selected another key, jabbed it into the cabinet's keyhole, and opened the door. Then he hurriedly placed his hand on the wrongly displayed tag and flipped it over. "It's from the 1940's. A good asking price—only a hundred dollars. Interested?"

"I don't think I'm ready to make a decision, quite yet. Could I see a set that's taller and has a design to it?"

"Of course." He walked back to the first cabinet and pulled out another pair of candlesticks, but they weren't the Harper set. "These here are from the 1920's and are eleven-inches tall," he said as he moved his hand up and down on the sticks. "Nice ornamental design running up and down the shafts, don't you think?" I nodded in agreement. "This seller is asking ninety-five dollars."

I showed my disinterest by stepping back a few steps from the case. "The price isn't really crucial as long as I know the set is one of a kind." I flipped my right hand at the candle—stick Glen was holding. "I don't want anything mass produced. I saw the same thing at an antique store in the Twin Cities just last week."

The guy remained in control and he wasn't put off by my attitude at all. He simply locked the candlesticks back in their display case, strolled past a couple more cases until he reached the final one, stopped in front of it, and then in a sincere tone said, "You know I think I have just the item you're looking for. These particular candlesticks were just put out for display yesterday. Silver-plated, very ornate and from the Victorian era."

Sounds like Violet Harper's set. If I'm not mistaken, the Victorian Era ran from 1837-1901. During the years 1810-1840 silver items took on heavier forms of decoration due to Egyptian, Greek, and Roman antiquities.

He posed a single candlestick in his left hand now. "See, I wasn't exaggerating when I said it was fancy. It has a square domed base that is laced with roses and vines, and the shaft is made up of two inverted bell sections with a knob centered between the bells. Dated 1839."

Paydirt finally, but I needed to remain calm. "Mmm … how tall would you say that is? My sister's chandelier hangs a little lower than the norm."

"I've got a tape measure in my pocket. Just let me set this down, and I'll get it out." He eased the candlestick onto a nearby table which was stacked with fancy dishes dating back to the 1950's. Now that his hands were free, he reached into his shirt pocket and pulled the measuring device out.

"Do you want me to hold one end for you?" I asked knowing he didn't require my help.

"Oh, no, I'm fine. This candlestick is exactly twelve and three-eighths inches tall. If you really want this set, the asking price is one-hundred and ninety-five dollars."

With fake excitement in my voice I said, "Yup, I think I've found exactly what I want. So is that price firm?" I asked.

"Yes, the price is very firm. The seller will not go any lower."

That's because the seller is you, Glen Wilson, I said to myself. I pulled my wallet out of my pant pocket hoping Glen would assume I was just getting my charge card ready, but what I was really reaching for was my business card. Now I flashed it in front of his face. "Sorry, nothing personal you understand, but I'm not buying the candlesticks for myself. You see a client of mine has authorized me to do it for her. Her husband took them when he ran out on her and her kids." I studied the guy as my information began to sink in. His face became ashen, and his body tightened like a bow. Scared as a rat! Probably thinks I plan to turn him into the cops. I suppose I could be nice and ease his worries. "Look," I said, "picture the candlesticks as simply icing on the cake. My main purpose in visiting Chubbs was to track down the devil-food-cake-guy—the missing husband. Since it's obvious to me you're not him, all I want to do is ask you a few questions. Is that all right?"

When Glen released a heavy sigh of relief, I half-expected one of the display cabinets to fall on top os us. "Oh, sure, sure, ask away, Mr. Malone. I have absolutely nothing to hide."

# CHAPTER 18

▼

"Dinosaurs are dead," my teacher said.
So how come I just saw one rear its ugly head.
Dirt and weeds were held in its tight grip.
And then I heard a voice, yell, "Let 'er rip."

The weather outside had changed dramatically during the time I spent indoors playing detective games. When I finally exited Chubbs with Violet Harper's candlesticks, the newly-arrived wind swiftly made its presence known, and it began fighting for ownership of my hair. Since I was too preoccupied with the flashing sign atop the bank building on the corner to care, I let it win. Maybe the meteorologists were right-the Twin Cities will get some much needed snow; the sign showed the temperature was thirty-degrees already.

The wind, along with the noticeable drop in temperature, chilled me to the bone. It pleased me to know the car was close at hand, but a minor adjustment needed to be made before scurrying there. I quickly unbuttoned my suit-coat, pulled the front flap over the left, pressed the candlesticks tightly against my mid-section, and then wrapped my arms around them. Umm, yes that helped some, I thought to myself as I ran across the street.

It turned out my hustling to the darn car was a lost cause. The door lock decided to be finicky. Of course, the only known remedy for curing the Topaz's lock problem was to apply the right pressure for about a minute and wait, so that's what I did and I finally got in. Now I laid Mrs. Harper's candlesticks on the unoccupied front passenger seat and quickly turned the key in the ignition. The car radio boldly advertised the time. It was already five p.m. I'd spent more time at Chubbs than I'd planned on, but at least it was fruitful. Once I shared a bit of my client's dilemma with Mr. Wilson, he really opened up; it probably helped that his one sister had gone through a similar situation.

His description of the man who sold him the candlesticks sounded a lot like Harper. Since I rather doubted Mr. Harper would've hired a middleman to take care of the sale for him—more risk of being caught—I showed Glen the 3 x 5 wedding picture of Harper when he was a mere eighteen-years-old. This was the only picture Violet could find of her husband. She said he hated having his picture taken—maybe he planned his escape a long time ago, who knows. At least Glen took his time studying it. Said he couldn't be positive since the guy had a beard, was much heavier and was obviously a lot older now.

"The guy I talked to came into Spinning Wheel Antiques in Hastings around the end of September, he said." Crap, I thought to myself, that must be a new store; it wasn't on my list when I sent out the flyers. "Seemed to be a very well-educated guy, around my age. Gave me a sob story about being unemployed and having five mouths to feed. 'Were the candlesticks worth much?' he asked. 'Did I think someone would be interested in purchasing them?' Sap that I am, I took them off his hands, but I did check out our hot list of stolen goods first. Not listed."

The car wasn't warmed up enough yet and would require a little more idling before I could leave town. I rubbed my hands together. Too bad I don't have any candles. I could stick them in the candleholders, light them and get some much needed heat. "Well, Violet, at least I got your family heirloom back."

When I arrived in Elk River earlier, there was no question about which path I would take to return to the cities. I make it a habit of returning via the same way I've come. But now as I sat passing the time, I felt compelled to change my routine. I was to take Highway 10 back to town instead. Was my quirky sixth sense responsible: premonitions? Perhaps.

The Topaz finally felt toasty so I shifted from park into drive and took off. Even though I rarely drive on Highway 10, I remembered it as a pretty straight road with very few bridges cutting through it, but I'd forgotten that in this particular area a whole fifteen minutes elapses before billboards or other advertisements begin spoiling the land. The first sign to destroy the clean look of the highway was a green, four-by-twelve metal one, and it was merely serving as a public announcement: five miles to Anoka—Halloween Capital of the World. There's another thing I need to add to my already long list of things to do before I die: attend Anoka's Halloween Parade.

Three seconds ticked by, four … another urge came over me, and I swung the car off Highway 10 to head north for parts unknown. Things were definitely out of kilt for me this evening, but why?

Unfortunately for me, the vast stretch of landscape on both sides of this road didn't furnish me with an answer. The only thing I did figure out for myself was that land developers and real estate vultures weren't lurking in the woods. Otherwise the land would be highly developed by now. A chunk of hair fell down over my left eye. I swiftly shoved it back, not wanting to miss a possible landmark. Just how much does a parcel of land go for out here, anyway? The way land's being scooped up these days, a person shopping at the right time could create a nice little nest egg for their future. Hmm....

Whoa! I was so deep in thought, planning how to make a killing in real estate, that I almost missed the change in scenery. Brown velvety cattails, bursting at the seams, were waving to me as well as leftover corn stalks and what appeared to be the remains of a street marker dangling from a wooden post. "Flamingo Way!" A crossroad appeared at this juncture, and again something advised me about which direction to take: a sharp right turn. As I left the road I had been traveling on, I mouthed the name of the street to imprint it on my brain. The name seemed vaguely familiar. Perhaps it was due to my past trip to Florida where flocks of bright pink birds, each poised on one leg, huddled around a watering hole in Disney World.

Wait a minute. My hands began tapping an old jazz tune on the steering wheel. Isn't that the name of the street where Evan's land donation is located? "Yes!" So why the heck am I being led to that area? The skull issue's been cleared up. That's what I hate about my special gift; I never know if the inklings I get are going to end up being worthwhile or not. Gift or curse, which will it end up being today, I wondered. All right, I'll play it out and see where this trip leads me.

The car lurched forward a bit before it came to a sudden halt in front of a sign that read "school under construction—keep out". I allowed my eyes to wander until I spotted the area where, only a couple months ago, Evan Cox presented his speech for the groundbreaking ceremony. The platform he stood on that day had been replaced by the new middle school's foundation as well as the building's outer shell. The building was already capped. In construction lingo that means the school was enclosed and winter work inside could proceed. I also noticed that a backhoe was still parked on the premises, but as far as I could tell it's cab was empty. Maybe it was just waiting to be removed and taken to a new sight.

Once I turned the car off though, I heard an extremely loud roar emanating from the backhoe and realized it was still in use. The operator must be hiding out in the Porta Pot, I thought, because this type of machinery simply doesn't run by itself.

Since I was obviously steered here for a reason, I figured I might as well get out of the car and check out the lay of the land originally owned by Evan Cox. I started my trudging along the front parcel of the property, nearest the car, allowing the absent worker plenty of time to see me so he or she wouldn't be so shocked by my presence. Sure enough, very shortly after I began my stroll, I spotted a male figure decked in work clothes standing at the front end of the backhoe, his back to me. Ah, that's why I didn't see him from the car: the angle of the machine hid him. So he wasn't in th Porta Pot after all.

The guy's actions were awfully strange. His arms flailed wildly at the sky as if he were giving referee opinions. I kind of felt like I was watching a live-animated cartoon show—but this was no cartoon show. Bees or rocks can easily create the kind of scene I was being privy to. Too late in the season for bees, I thought to myself, must be rocks. I revved up my middle-aged body and raced towards him at top speed.

The worker must've sensed someone was approaching him because he spun around and hollered, "Hurry up, I need help!"

"I know," I yelled, and then hastily cast my eyes on the only two-piece suit I owned. Oh, heck, being a good Samaritan far outweighs the importance of keeping one's suit from getting soiled. Besides, ever since I saw Rod Thompson, a neighbor of mine who works for the FBI, wearing that gray three-piece wool suit of his, I've been telling myself to break down and buy another one. So if I throw caution to the wind—I'll have no more valid excuses for not purchasing it. Of course, just as I resolved this situation to my satisfaction, temporary sanity kicked in. I know the way I do things, and so it could be another two years before I found myself entering a JC Penney store. As I passed the cab of the CAT, I pulled my suit jacket off and tossed it through the doorway.

"What's going on?" I finally inquired when I was standing shoulder to shoulder with the troubled machine operator. Oh, oh! I'd seen this guy before. My stomach immediately twisted into a double knot as anger flared up from within. All I could hope for was that my facial expression didn't give me away. This was the guy who made a pass at Rita when we were at the Heritage Festival. The day it happened I wanted to search for him in the crowd and beat him to pulp, and now that I've found him I can't slug him because I can't afford a law suit. Where's the justice in this world?

There's no other way to describe Ron than to say he looks like Minnesota's popular lumberjack legend, Paul Bunyan; red and black plaid shirt, blue stocking cap, high-top steel-toed safety boots. All that was missing was his sidekick—Babe the Blue Ox, and as far as I knew the likeness of that animal was still up in Brainerd staring out at Highway 371. "I dug something up," he finally shared. "I just need someone to help me get it out of the way."

Fighting to keep my temper in check, I bit my bottom lip and said what had come to mind earlier, "Rocks in your path, huh?" One of the main complaints you hear from Minnesota farmers is that rocks really disrupt their field work and do a great deal of damage to their machinery.

"Heck no, just bones."

"Animal?" I hurriedly questioned.

Paul Bunyan's look alike said, "Mister, I'm no scientist, but I'd say human."

"So how many bones are we talking about?"

"The whole enchilada."

A complete skeleton, I thought to myself. Then without thinking I said outloud, "I suppose it could be part of that skull prank, huh?"

Ron eyed me suspiciously. "Say, are you a reporter? Because if you are, I'm not saying another word."

"Hey, don't get all excited," I said. "I'm not a reporter, just a friend of the Cox family." I figured Ron didn't need to know about my being a PI.

The big guy's defenses dropped, and his relaxed attitude returned. "Oh? Just wanted to see how the school was progressing, huh?" When he reached the hole where the object was resting he shoved his plaid shirt sleeves up about four inches above his wrist bone, then he jumped into the dug out area.

I assumed I wasn't needed in the hole too, so I squatted near the edge to help with the resurrection. "That and I had some work in this area too," I replied nonchalantly. "You know when I pulled up I was surprised to see the CAT still here, especially since the school is capped."

"Yeah, normally it wouldn't still be here, but another rich family in the area just donated a ton of money for a greenhouse addition to the school. So my boss calls and gives me orders to dig up the ground where that's going. They want the cement floor poured before winter sets in."

He begins to hoist the skeleton up to me now. "You know I've been thinking about that dumb skull I found. That middle school science teacher must've been one hell of a prankster, huh?"

"Yup, but I'd say he's not laughing much these days." I grabbed the head and shoulders of the skeleton, Ron the feet, and we set it on the level ground.

Ron took his stocking cap off and scratched his head. "Why do you say that?"

"Oh, I heard the Anoka-Hennepin School Board decided his joke was too costly for the school district. They fired him." Once the equipment driver was out of the hole and standing parallel with me, we carried his discovery to a flat area where a thick cluster of trees remained and set it down. It was there that I noticed one of the crumpled hands was hiding something. "Guess what? It looks like your new find is bearing a gift."

The man standing alongside me swiped his snow-moistened forehead with his dirt-encrusted hand. "Well, that ain't my concern. Let someone else decide what it means. I'm on a tight schedule,"he said. "I gotta get moving."

Hmm ... I guess I'm going to have to be pretty persuasive if I want to get down in that hole and search for more clues before I leave. "Right," I replied as I slyly edged toward the open ground. "I hear you; time's money. Tell you what, I'll buzz the cops for you if you'll just let me take a couple minutes to see if anything else might be hiding down there," I said pointing to where the skeleton was found.

"I'll give you five minutes, mister. Then you gotta clear out of here. Me and the backhoe got work to do."

I glanced at my wristwatch. "That should be plenty."

# CHAPTER 19

▼

As soon as I unlocked the door to my apartment, I discovered that Gracie had major issues; she was pacing frantically. Since I've been a dog owner for a considerable amount of time now, there was no need to decipher what she was trying to communicate. "All right, simmer down girl," I said as I rubbed her back with my hands. "Your message is coming through loud and clear. I just want a second to change. Okay?"

"Wuff! Wuff!"

I yanked the key out of the keyhole and went straight to the bedroom to hunt for a pair of jeans and a flannel shirt. The shirt was hanging in the closet, but the pants were on the floor where I'd last dropped them collecting dust. When I squatted down to pick up the pants I noticed that my answering machine was blinking wildly. "Shoot!" No time to listen to the message—can't afford to have the dog do her duty in here. I stepped into the pants, tossed on my shirt, and went back to the hallway where Gracie was still waiting for me. I quickly grabbed her leash, and we were on our way, or so I thought.

Mrs. Grimshaw just happened to be opening her door as I closed mine. She spotted Gracie first, and immediately reached out to pat her. "Hi Gracie. Oh, hi Matt. Where have you been hiding? It's been a couple weeks since I've seen you." Before I could respond to her question, she continued, "And how's your father doing?"

"My father's doing fine. Thanks for asking." The mutt wanted out of the building now, not two minutes from now. She tugged on her leash and began whining. "Sorry, Margaret, I'd like to chat but as you see I can't. Gracie's about to piddle any second." More whining. "Shush, Gracie." I started to lead her towards the stairwell. "How about if I stop in after the dog's finished with her rounds?"

"Oh, yes, that would be wonderful," my neighbor said as she squeezed her ninety-one-year-old hands together, "Matt, how would you like to join me for supper then."

Bachelor that I am, I never turn down a dinner invitation if I can help it. "Sure," I replied as I opened the door. "See you in a little while." As the dog and I raced down the steps, I said in a hushed tone, "Gotta hand it to you girl. You sure get me a lot of free meals."

Margaret's dining room table, as well as the rest of her apartment, was decorated for the next holiday on the calendar: Thanksgiving. "You're involved in so many activities outside of this apartment," I said. "When do you find the time to decorate?" The only holiday I ever manage to decorate for is Christmas, and that's done around the tenth hour on Christmas Eve right after I've had a couple mugs of Hot Toddy. Then up goes the wreath and the artificial tree.

"Oh, it's all in the planning, Matt," Margaret said as she pointed to her forehead which was covered with gray-washed hair. "All in the planning. My mother always said plan ahead so you get things done on time."

"Smart mom."

"Yes, she was, but it also helps to have a ton of those new-fangled freezer storage containers on hand that all the grocery stores sell too."

I sniffed the aromas floating through the dining area. Tonight there was no hint of Margaret's specialty: spaghetti. "So can I retrieve anything from the kitchen for you?"

"Mr. Malone, how many times do I have to repeat myself? When you are a guest in my home, I serve you. Now, just sit down and I'll be right back." My neighbor gently pushed me towards the table and then hurried off to her kitchen from where she returned from quite quickly with a tray of assorted foods. "We'll start with the salad, first," she said as she handed me my prepared portion and then sat down.

"Say, is Petey all right? I haven't heard him since I got here."

She lifted her head to face me. "See, I knew you really liked Petey." I winced at her comment. "Don't worry, there's no need to be alarmed. He's only off visiting a lady friend."

"Oh? Now he's being used for mating services?"

It must've been the tone of my voice rather than the question that made Margaret's face turn beet-red and the answer to follow sound a bit defensive. "Well, how else do you think this senior citizen gets spending money?"

I shrugged my shoulders and glanced down at the plate in front of me. Stupid me. Another foot in mouth dilemma. I should have never made such a comment to a person I know is very sensitive. How do I resolve this? All I could think of for a remedy was to turn the conversation in another direction. The tip of my fork lightly touched what was waiting to be eaten. "Hmm ... this is very interesting. I've never had a mushroom appetizer before. Do I need to add any seasoning?"

Margaret's lips displayed a smidgen of a smile. "Actually, you're eating a mushroom salad, and no, there's no need to season it. Oregano, salt, pepper, cloves, and lime juice have already been mixed in."

I took a bite and then I reached for the warm sliced bread that was tucked in a blue oval basket. "You're right. The salad is really tasty. So is it another recipe from your village in the *old country*?" I asked.

My neighbor waved her free hand over the table. "Heaven's no! About a year ago, I attended a community education class dealing with Italian cooking. Mama D was the instructor: a wonderful cook and a great inspiration. Why, do you know she didn't start her first restaurant business in Dinkytown near the University of Minnesota until her husband passed away. And several years later after the first place was a huge success, she opened many more restaurants in the Twin Cities area." She slid her fork under her mushrooms and tried to keep them balanced till they reached her mouth.

"Wow!" I patted my mouth with a turkey designed napkin. "I've never heard that story even though I've eaten in her Dinkytown eatery many times."

Margaret set her fork down for a minute. "Well, now you know, but enough about Mama D. Let's talk about your father, Matt." She reached across the table and softly touched my hand that was picking up another piece of bread.

I placed the bread on my plate after she pulled her hand away and then rested a hand on each side of my empty salad plate. "Well, when he first came home from the hospital, my siblings and I were really worried he wouldn't stick to his doctor's orders."

"Is he?"

"Yes, thank God."

"You should be thankful. It's very hard for people to change habits that have been hanging around for fifty years or more. A person really needs a considerable amount of willpower to move on to a new way of life."

"Exactly," I said jiggling the glass of water Margaret had provided for me, "and my dad certainly has that."

My neighbor was finally finished with her salad so now she said, "Please excuse me. It's time to get the main course."

"Of course," I stood and pulled her chair out for her.

"I hope you like Chicken Cacciatore because that's what we're having."

"Chicken and I get along just fine," I said in a raised voice directed towards the kitchen. Heck that's mostly what I eat at my place. Chickens cheap and easy to doctor: honey-glazed, barbecued, coated, and creamed.

"Here it is, and as you can see I've made plain buttered noodles to accompany it." She set the platter down and sat again. "You know with all the talking we've been doing Matt, there'ssomething you still haven't mentioned yet."

"What's that?" I cautiously asked.

"Work, my boy, work." She passed the chicken and noodles to me.

I set the platter down next to my plate and took two pieces of chicken and a couple spoonfuls of noodles. "I haven't mentioned work because I've had pretty slim pickin's lately. As a matter of fact, ever since Cox cancelled my job for him, I've been putting all my eggs in one basket. It isn't a big basket, but I'd like to close it out by the end of the year depending on how lucky I am." I was referring to the Harper case of course.

"I saw you leaving the building around three or so, today, all dressed up in your finest. Did that have something to do with this one case or a funeral?"

"The case I'm trying to crack."

Margaret coughed. "Sorry, I guess I didn't chew my meat up good enough." She took a sip of water. "Speaking of cracking cases, I don't think I ever told you how terrible I felt when your job for Evan Cox fell through—I know that would've been another fine feather in your cap."

I reached out and patted Margaret's slender hand. She had so much compassion for others. "That's okay. I'm not really a cap person. Besides, in my line of business you get some you lose some." Now I released her hand and popped a small piece of chicken in my mouth. Oh man, so tender and delicious. Too bad this little Italian woman is way beyond my years, otherwise I'd be proposing about now. Instead, I swallowed my meat and said, "Since you brought Evan's name into the picture, maybe you'd be interested in hearing what took place after my important meeting today."

"Yes, of course," she replied, her eyes ablaze like hundred-watt bulbs."

"When I left what I was doing in Elk River, I decided to come back to the Twin Cities via Highway 10 not the route I took to get there. That alone was strange."

"Your sixth sense acting up again, huh?"

"Yeah, I'm pretty sure. Well, anyway, after about fifteen minutes on highway 10 I veered off to a road I've never heard of."

"What was the name?"

"I don't know. It doesn't matter. What matters is the next turn I took."

"Yes?"

I took a bite of noodles before I continued. They were getting cold. "The street sign for this road said Flamingo Way." I looked at Margaret's face to see if there was any recognition. There didn't seem to be any. So I asked, "Does the name ring any bells for you?"

"Mmm ... vaguely," she sweetly replied as she added honey to her cup of tea. "Where should I know it from—some show we saw together?"

"It'll come to you. Anyway, the darn Topaz began acting up as soon as I came upon this huge piece of land that had been cleared out in the middle of nowhere.

My elderly hostess immediately brought her bird like hands to her mouth. "No! You're not saying your sixth sense brought you to the land Evan donated for the school project?"

"Yes, that's exactly what I'm saying," I quickly answered. "And get this, the CAT operator just happened to discover more body parts right before I arrived on the scene."

Margaret sighed. "Remains of the first joke I suppose."

"I don't think so. Too much time has elapsed between the finding of the skull and the bones. Plus, this one was in a different location, one originally not intended to be dug up. Here's the wildest part, the bones actually make up a full skeleton and a tiny secret was hidden in one hand."

My neighbor's brows twisted tightly. "Something tells me that Evan Cox or Harold Sinclair will be calling you shortly, and it's not my sixth sense."

"We'll see."

"Yes indeedy, you'll see. Your detective work for Evan is back on the front burner again, of that I'm certain," she said as she clapped her hands together in a joyful manner.

# CHAPTER 20

▼

The message came swifter than either Margaret or I could have ever imagined. A total of six messages were waiting for me when I got back to my abode, the first of which was from Harold Sinclair. "Matt, I just got off the phone with the fella in charge at the middle school construction site. Something else has turned up. Please call me as soon as possible. Thanks."

I ignored the other five messages. Harold's required top priority at the moment. I quickly picked up my notepad that rested by the phone and paged through it until I found exactly what I was looking for: phone numbers of the Anoka-Hennepin School Board members.

As I concentrated on the ringing of the phone on the other end, Gracie sauntered over to where I was sitting, sniffed me up and down, and then immediately began clawing me. "What do you want?" I asked her rather harshly, not liking the fact that she was disturbing me. "We were out just two hours ago." I searched my pant pockets till I found a dog biscuit. "Here," I tossed the biscuit on the unmade bed. "Now go snack on that for awhile. I'm busy."

"Pardon me?" Harold said in a slightly raised tone of voice. "Go snack on what? Well, I never—you've got the wrong number fella." Harold slammed his phone down and my ear almost exploded.

With no other way of communicating with Harold, I immediately re-dialed his number. Luckily he picked up on the first ring. "Harold, it's Matt Malone."

"Well, it's certainly a pleasure to hear your voice, Matt. I just hung up on a crank call and was prepared to do so again."

Hmm, should I be nice and tell him that caller was me, I wondered, or let him think what he wanted? Honesty won out. "Ah, actually that other call wasn't a crank one. That was me."

"You? Really?" Harold said in a stunned voice. "Don't you think your phrase 'snack on that' was a strange way to begin a conversation?"

"Sorry, about that. The mutt was being a pest so I figured a treat would do the trick."

Harold's baritone laugh was so hearty it vibrated my phone. "Dogs! I understand how trying they can be. Duke, our new dog, always acts like he doesn't get enough attention from us."

The length of the day was finally wearing on me. I stretched my one free arm. "So, Harold, what's up—your message didn't clue me in?"

"Well, apparently a skeleton was dug up on the school property, but of course you already know that. From what I've heard, you were in the vicinity when it was uncovered and reported the find to the police."

"That's right." What direction was this conversation taking, I wondered. Where money finds its way into my pockets, maybe?

"Matt," Harold's voice mellowed a notch now, "I know we told you adios when we thought we didn't need you anymore, but with this new find, well, Evan said we need to retain your services again. Do you happen to be available?"

I stared at the one lone file folder sitting on my desk and decided to take a risk—go out on a limb. I'll usually do that if I know I can get more money. Let's see. The December rent is due, and Christmas is just around the corner. No big crisis. This PI has come to the conclusion that he should fake non-interest anyway. "Geez, I don't know. I've got three or four cases that are demanding almost all of my attention, Harold."

"Mr. Cox will definitely make it worth your while."

"Oh, I ... I don't know."

Harold cleared his throat. "Look, Evan said if you weren't sure you wanted to take this job, I was supposed to drop Neil Welch's name."

I sucked in the stale air. "Let me take a quick look at my appointment book, Harold. Maybe I can swing it." I cradled the phone under my chin and then opened my book and flipped the pages back and forth for a second; I didn't feel it was necessary for Rita's uncle to know how little business I had. Time is up. I moved the phone back into conversational position again. "Yeah, okay. I guess I can squeeze in research for Evan."

"Great!" Harold blasted back. "When can you start?"

I yawned. "Friday work for you?"

"Perfect. Now, there's one more personal matter I need to take up with you. Vivian wants to know when you and our lovely niece are going to come for dinner."

I ran my hand through my hair. "Geez, I don't know, Harold. It's so hard to pin Rita down whenever she's working on a huge marketing project, but I'll see what I can do. I'm known to have some very persuasive charms."

"Ah, yes," Harold mumbled. "From what I've heard, you can be pretty persuasive even without the charm."

This time I almost ate the phone as I yawned. "What? I didn't catch what you said."

Rita's uncle coughed. "Oh, I just said I'll pass on to Viv what you said. Now, Matt, don't forget to call me if you need any cash flow for the research."

# CHAPTER 21

▼

Clever me. I never shared with anyone that I did more skull research, on the side, right after learning about the big joke the science teacher pulled. See, I'm the type of PI who feels it doesn't do any harm to stash pertinent information in the old memory bank because somewhere along the road I'll more than likely be called upon to use it. What's even better about the continued research is that I got sidetracked and revisited the bones display as well. And boy, did I take notes. So guess what, Harold. I lied about Friday; my research has already begun.

Just as I went over to the desk in my bedroom and began digging through all the notes strewn across it, the ringing phone trapped me. Of course, not having caller ID, I had no way of knowing whether the person on the other end was selling something or looking for help, so after the third nagging ring I picked up. The decision was a wise one since the caller was Rita. Shocked to hear her voice during the busiest season of the year for her employer, I yanked the chair away from the desk and sat down. "Geez, I can't believe you actually found some spare time to call. You must be caught up, huh?"

"If only that were true," Rita replied in a disgusted tone, not at all the way she normally speaks. "You can't imagine how many times I've wanted to drop everything and hightail it over to your place instead."

"Really? What's stopping you then?" I gently teased as I picked up a pen and played with it.

"Can't afford to get fired, Matt. You know I haven't built up enough seniority yet."

I wondered why she called then if she still didn't have time to squeeze me into her busy schedule, but I didn't dare ask. "So are you at least eating decently and getting enough sleep?" I already knew the answer to my questions, but I waited to see if she would be honest with me.

A heavy sigh reached my ear. "No and no. Look, this is going to be short and to the point. As it is, I snuck out to use a phone in the hallway so my boss won't think I'm goofing off."

"Okay, shoot. What is it you want to say?"

"Matt, I feel awful about this—but I can't go to your parents' house for Thanksgiving."

I took a pen from the desk and began twirling it. "Someone else gave you a better offer, huh?"

"No," she laughed softly. "An uncle of my dad's isn't doing well, so my parents and I are driving to North Dakota to visit him. We're leaving this Wednesday evening."

"Oh? Well, don't fret. The Malone clan will see to it that I'm well occupied while you're gone." I scratched my head with my free hand, trying to think of something I was supposed to ask her. It finally came to me. "Rita, your uncle Harold has been bugging me again about when we are coming to dinner. Do you think there's a chance we can fit that in soon?" I set the pen down and crossed my fingers, hoping she'd say what I wanted to hear.

"Actually, the week after this looks pretty clear."

"Ah, there you are, Rita," an unfamiliar voice said. "We've been looking all over for you. You're wanted on line two."

"Gotta go," Rita hurriedly said and then she whispered, "Matt, you know I love you a bunch."

"Ditto." I hung the phone up and ran my hand through my hair. "Dang it!" Gracie jumped off the bed where she had been resting and snuggled up to where I was sitting. She was trying to comfort me in dog fashion. "I thought Rita and I finally were going to connect, Gracie. I can't believe how many things get in the way of our relationship."

I pushed the chair back too hard, and the legs snagged on the carpet. "Great! What else can go wrong?"

Upset as I was about Rita's and my not getting together, it didn't take me long to return to what I was doing, before her phone call, but after searching through several piles of notes, all I discovered was how much accumulated junk needed to be tossed. If anyone took the time to really examine the rooms of my home, they'd say I was a good candidate for an organization specialist. Of course, I'd never hire one. I can't afford to pay for the service on my crazy income and besides, I don't like people rifling through my things. "Where are those darn notes I took on the skull and bones, anyhow?" As I continued flipping through more sheets of paper I thought I heard a funny noise. "Did you hear that Gracie?" I questioned without looking down at her. Could it be a mouse? It certainly was the right time of year for them to come into a dwelling.

The strange sound stopped, and then it began again. It seemed to be coming from the floor near the desk. I glanced down at Gracie and discovered what was causing the noise. Her feet were parading back and forth on half-sheets of typing paper that had obviously fallen off the desk at some point in time.

The dog must have sensed I was watching her. She stopped what she was doing, looked up into my eyes and said, "Wuff, wuff."

"Gracie! Move those big feet of yours so I can see what you're standing on." The mutt swiftly reacted to my orders lifting one back a couple inches, then the other.

With the dog out of my way now, I stooped, retrieved what was on the carpet and stood again. The papers were a little crumpled but I was still able to scan the notes that I had been searching for. One particular sentence really caught my attention. It contained a local coroner's comments in regards to finding a body in a wooded area. "Whenever a body's found in a wooded location, it's very suspicious." Even though the remark made perfect sense, it didn't sit well with me. Why? Because it meant the cops and other law enforcement officials would be swarming around the school site and the skeleton for a long, long time; a DNA study takes several weeks, and mitochondria testing takes many months.

I dropped the notes on the desk to mix with the rest of the mess. No bones analysis by specialists was going to stop this PI from doing his job. I've got connections in all the right places. Now I went over to the radio sitting on the small table by the bed and clicked it on. My favorite station would be giving the weather forecast any minute and I also wanted to hear if there was still some spin with the skeleton.

# CHAPTER 22

▼

The youthful male voice on Minnesota Public Radio said, "The last piece of music you heard, *Buffalo Dance*, was first performed by the Zuni pueblo Indians in 1953." That Indian song, which slid through the airwaves right after the news, finally woke me from my ineptitude. It drew me in and inspired me. I was so pumped that I wanted to beat my own drums—Evan Cox had created a new mission for me.

As I leaned over to turn the radio off, the cuff of my long-sleeve shirt caught the edge of a very dusty book resting beside it: the one about Dakota Indians. If I'd taken the time to read the latest addition to my Indian book collection like I kept saying I was going to do, that much dust wouldn't have accumulated. I swiped my hand across the jacket for a quick clean. "Ah choo!" Oops, time to drag the dust rag out. "Ooh! Ah!" My stomach muscles suddenly tightened—like when my sixth sense is about to kick in. "Thanks, Aunt Fiona." I'd inherited this stupid curse from her.

My hands found their way to my mid-section and rested there. I gotta get back on track. Otherwise I won't get anything accomplished. "Ouch! Crap!" All right, maybe I'll just flip through the pages of the book to see if there's the slightest hint of a connection between it and the job for Evan. If not, it's back to reality. I released one hand from my stomach and used it to grasp the spine of the new book. Once I had a firm hold on it, I hastily fanned the pages using my thumb. Nope, there didn't appear to be any relationship between my curse and the book. Evidently my assumption at the time of purchase was indeed correct, this book was for future reference only.

But why did the sharp pain persist then? Could it be I'm having an appendicitis attack and not a sixth sense jolt? No way. My body was made of iron. I t wasn't designed for necessary hospital stays. I left the bedroom for the kitchen where I generously poured myself a steaming cup of coffee and added a spoonful of sugar. Over the years I've found that when I create enough spinning in my coffee mug, the swirling motion becomes a relaxing force for me. I was hoping it would do that for me now.

After a few seconds, the swishing hot coffee finally made me relaxed enough that my mind went back to a few days before when I helped Ron move the skeleton out of the hole. I wish I knew what the object was that was crushed in the skeleton's hand. There was no way of recognizing it; the 2" x 3" article was heavily caked with layers of dirt. A small item such as that could've been a coin purse, but coin purses generally don't have straps attached to them. Hmm … it will be interesting to hear what time period the forensic team comes up with. If the skeleton dates back to the 19$^{th}$ century, perhaps the item was used for trade purposes. I picked up my mug and took a few sips of coffee. The specific time frame definitely gave me more to ponder.

After a another generous helping of coffee, the pain in my stomach subsided. Of course, as soon as Gracie noticed I wasn't as tense, she walked over to my chair and begged for a milkbone. I retrieved one from the cupboard and tossed it to her. It was then that I realized I was getting way ahead of myself. What if the skeleton ends up being an animal? Ron and I just assumed it was human. Remember what your notes said, Matt. The decomposition rate of bone can often times cause a person to think that the bones are human when they are really animal. Luckily modern scientific advances can make that determination.

I left my mug by the coffee pot and went to the phone and dialed a number I've had for awhile. "Hello, Mr. Cox, this is Matt Malone. I was wondering if you'd have time to gather all your ancestors' diaries for me if they're handy. I was thinking of coming by this afternoon to pick them up."

"Why sure, Matt. I'll have Claire get them out of storage," Evan replied, "but I don't know what you think you'll find in them. Margaret, Harold, Claire, and I went through them when the skull was first discovered on the property."

"Yes, I'm well aware of that. I just thought I'd take another stab at it and see if anything of significance jumps out at me."

Evan cleared his throat. "It can't hurt, I guess. So what time do you think you might get here?"

I turned and looked at the clock on the stove. "In about an hour."

"Oh?" Evan said, his voice displaying disappointment. "I won't get to see you then. I'm leaving for a meeting in fifteen minutes, but I know Claire will be delighted to see you again."

Oh, wonderful! Just what my heart's been yearning for—time alone with his wife, Claire.

# CHAPTER 23

▼

After some deep thinking on my part, I finally thought of a way not to see Claire Cox by myself. Simply ask Claire's garden pal, Margaret Grimshaw, to come along.

Boy, when I called my apartment neighbor and invited her to go for a short car ride, you'd think I had sent her straight to heaven. I mean I've never heard another living soul so ecstatic. But then again, who else do I know that's been cooped up for several days in a little apartment with a ornery parrot named Petey?

"So exactly why are we visiting Evan's house, Matt? You never did say. Have the police uncovered more bones on the school property?"

I shifted my gaze slightly from the road to Margaret who was sitting beside me in the Topaz. "Not that I'm aware of. Although, I do plan to call one of my police buddies and see what he's heard through the grapevine."

The petite Italian woman clapped her gloved hands together. "Good. I like that plan. Then you can share with me."

"Sorry, I'm not at liberty to divulge everything I find out. Some things just have to remain under the covers."

A girlish laughter spilled through the car. "Oh, Matt, you take me way too seriously. I know you can't share all your information with me. I just wanted to sneak that in there."

"Well, now wait a minute." I cupped my head to the right side. That comment of yours is making me do a little soul searching.

I could really use your assistance with a bit of research, later today, if you're interested."

Margaret's almost invisible eyebrows nearly took flight. "Me? But what could I possibly do for you?"

I unbuttoned the top button of my winter coat. "Remember those family diaries you looked through at Evan and Claire's?" She nodded. "Well, Evan's giving them to me so I can examine them more closely."

"Why would you want to waste time reading them? We didn't find anything helpful in them."

"I'm going with my gut instincts on this one. I think there's direct mention of this skeleton that's been uncovered—but not in the way one would think—the remains aren't a relative of Evan's but rather a visitor to the old homestead."

Margaret sat up straighter. "So, you don't suspect foul play, then?"

"I'm not saying yay or nay," I replied, "but the few minutes I studied the skeleton, there didn't appear to be any evidence of it."

# CHAPTER 24

▼

It was a little past nine-thirty when I finally realized I wouldn't be getting any-more work out of Margaret. Her eye-lids were doing such a dramatic rapid-paced dance that I decided to call it a day and pack up the leftovers from our Kentucky Fried Chicken meals. Since I didn't know what my plans were for supper the next night, I placed the packaged leftovers in Margaret's delicate hands along with her share of the diaries and sent her on her sleepy way. I guess it was okay that we quit when we did because before we began reading we'd made a pact that we'd each read only two diaries this evening, and we had accomplished that task.

Now that my apartment was void of my neighbor, I returned to the couch where I placed my back against one of its sloping arms and pivoted my aver-aged-sized legs across the seat cushions. Hmm, I'll be darn. This made for a pretty comfy way to study. Why the heck didn't I do this earlier? Oops, I guess I should've chosen my beefy manly Lazy-Boy chair to recline in. The mutt who dominates this particular abode thought it was time to join her owner.

Of course, Gracie didn't wait for her master's permission to climb aboard, she just jumped on the other end of the sofa and laid down.

How dare she invade my privacy like that? I was peeved. This was my couch, and I wanted it all to myself. Remembering what my neighbor's eyelids looked like only a few moments before, I moved my feet almost as fast, thinking the dog would take the subtle hint. She didn't. As a matter of fact, she raised her elon-gated head and quickly dropped it on my size-eleven socks covered feet. Well, goody goody. At least she'll get what she deserves: stinky feet in her face.

Mrs. Grimshaw may be tucked in for the night, I thought, but there's no way I'm falling asleep anytime soon. I was running on four cups of strong black coffee and two-count them-two glasses of wine. I'm ready for an all-nighter. Five diaries to read through and then I can relax. At dawn when everyone is waking up and my circuits have finally shorted out, I'll just crash. Now I set four of the unread diaries on the floor within easy reach, and placed the fifth one in front of my face.

As I began perusing the third diary, I found it was very similar to the first two I had read when Margaret was still here: boring as hell. Let me be so kind as to share a snippet with you.

> *Thursday—Mother's day to join her ladies circle at church, for their usual quilting bee. Papa's finished his morning chores so he and Tommy went fishing. They hope to catch enough fish for supper. Ambrose and Archie are off to lend the neighbor a hand with farm chores. His son fell last week and broke his leg, so he's no help. And me, why I'm keeping myself busy darning socks and ironing the clothes we will wear to Sunday services.*

Nearing midnight, I left the couch twice, once to get a snack and then to adjust the temperature in the room. Sometime shortly after twelve, my body gave out on the couch and I nodded off to sleep. The only thing I recall, before my eyes actually closed, is diary number four being lifted to the couch in slow motion and then being plopped on my chest.

# CHAPTER 25

▼

Early this morning I received an extraordinary invite, one that I wasn't about to refuse. That meant the diaries would have to wait. A good friend of mine, Doctor Raines, called and asked if I'd like to go on a short excursion with him to the town of Anoka. Hmm, I thought to myself, what a coincidence that I'd be asked to return to a town that I just recently drove through. I didn't share this information with my friend though. I simply allowed him to continue his tale.

According to Doc, the Anoka County Coroner needed his expert advice. Theodore, Ted for short, said that as soon as heard the exact nature of the business he immediately thought of me. Since he didn't go into further details on the phone, I didn't know if his remark should be construed as good news or bad news.

Ted, one of Minnesota's homegrown farmboys, happens to be the head of the Anthropology Department at the University of Minnesota as well as a highly respected world-wide author in the scientific realm. And in addition to being an anthropologist, he has a forensic science background.

I knew the professor as a habitually punctual person, so I planned to be waiting on the street outside the Foley no later than ten minutes before he was expected to arrive. The clock in the kitchen now read seven-twenty, just five minutes to gulp down a cup of coffee and lace up my dress shoes. On my way towards the door the mutt brushed up against my legs. "No time for playing, girl. You're on your own again, so just be good and take a nap."

Gracie's head dusted the floor when she answered with her usual, "Wuff,"and then she made a hasty retreat to the bedroom.

I plucked a notepad off the hallway table right before locking up. After making sure the door was secure, I made a mad dash to the fourth floor exit door and stairwell. As I jogged down the carpeted steps I managed to peer at my wrist-watch. I had one minute to reach the main floor and skedaddle out the door, that's if there's no interference like there usually is. Lucky me, when I entered the main lobby there was no one about, but my sixty seconds were up. I flew through the complex's front double-hung doors and was out on the street.

A hot-red Corvette pulled up to the curb just as my feet touched the public sidewalk. Could it be Ted already? I stooped down and looked through the window at the driver. Yup, it's him. I opened the passenger door and slid in. "Good-morning."

"Ditto, Matt. Ted looked at me from every angle before we departed. "Wow, you sure haven't changed since I last saw you. That was about two years ago, wasn't it?"

I studied what I was wearing. "Right. I was working on a cold case at the time," and probably clothed in the same suit, I didn't add.

"Oh, yes, the Hutton murder if I recall."

"Yup. What a memory you have." Now that I was buckled in I lovingly spread my hands across the Corvette's dashboard. "Ted, how come this little baby hasn't been put to bed, yet? You usually store it in your friend's pole barn around the end of October."

"Yeah, I know. I caught your slight hesitation about whether you should hop in the car or not." He slapped his steering wheel and then let out a strapping laugh. "My friend, since old age started spinning its wheels in front of me, I've begun a counter attack—increase the usage of the Corvette—reduce the storage time."

"I'm only going to say one thing in response to your new thinking," I said. "Don't remember my phone number when you're stranded in three-feet of snow sometime." I turned my head to take a good look at the professor now, a classy guy, always a sharp dresser. I envy men like him. Today he was wearing a brown flannel suit with a cream-colored shirt and a dark brown necktie that had minute flecks of gold thread running through it. The color of his clothing blended well with his washed out brown wavy hair. He sure didn't look a day over sixty. "You know, Ted, I don't think old age is anywhere near your doorstep, but for the record, just how old are you?"

His baritone response came a lot faster than I anticipated. "Sixty-five, next month."

"See," I said, "like I thought, you're still a young pup."

"Coming from you, I'll accept that," he said.

"Good, but remember to be as kind to me when I turn sixty-five." I turned my attention to the highway now and caught the newest road signs; we were already nearing Champlin which borders on Anoka. Only ten minutes left of our ride. "Ah, Ted, don't you think it's time to tell me what this trip to Anoka's all about?"

"You know Matt, I did plan to fill you in on the way here, but I've changed my mind. I want you to be surprised."

One of my pet peeves is being kept in the dark, and internally I was having a cat fit. "Okay," I replied in an even tone as if it didn't bother me in the least. Ted was lucky I trusted his judgement implicitly because there aren't too many people I can make that statement about. Nope, if this friend thinks it's necessary to drag me along for something related to his work, he's absolutely positive the trip's going to be beneficial to me also

My friend made a sharp right off of Highway 169 onto Anoka's Main Street, and three blocks later he made a left at the light and then drove straight for another two blocks. Upon entering the parking lot of the Anoka County Coroner's office, he playfully announced, "Here we are, Matt. You are now in Anoka, the Halloween Capital of the World. I hope you brought your costume."

I smartly replied, "Ted, you're a month late. This is November. You need to update your calendar. Thanksgiving is just around the corner." It sure was strange ending up in this town twice in one month. What was bringing me here this time, I wondered.

We entered the building together, but then I waited a distance back while Ted announced to the receptionist that he was there for a meeting. The young woman behind the counter spoke so loudly that I heard her say that she'd let Dr. Russell know we were here and in the meantime we should help ourselves to their wonderful literature on the coffee table as well as the free coffee and cookies.

As soon as the word food was mentioned I propelled myself in that direction, opposite of where Ted was standing. Hmm, chocolate cookies, what a smart way to start the day. Every office should have the same offering. After I placed a few cookies in my napkin, I turned to my doctor friend and asked, "Would you like me to grab some for you, too?"

Ted waved his hand. "No thanks. Way too early for me."

"Suit yourself," then I dropped myself in the nearest chair.

I only had time to devour two cookies and a half-cup of coffee when Doctor Russell finally made his presence known by clearing his throat. "Ah hmm." After quickly studying us both from the top of our heads to our shoes, he bypassed me and walked straight to Ted. Either my friend's suit was a dead give away or he was merely recognized due to his picture being shown so frequently in the scientific world. I'd like to think it was the latter.

A genuine smile flashed across his face before he said, "Dr. Raines, I'm Dr. James Russell, but I prefer that you call me Jim." The slim, thirty-something gentleman, wearing a white lab coat, presented his hand to Ted. "I appreciate your coming on such short notice."

"Well, thanks for the invite," my friend replied evenly, "and I like to go by Ted. I'm not much for formalities unless of course there are students around." Dr. Russell snickered. "The two of us are looking forward to seeing your new facilities and the item you called me about." Now he craned his neck towards me. "By the way, meet Matt Malone."

Jim acted genuinely pleased to meet me. He extended his muscular hand towards me and I took it. "Mr. Malone, what a nice surprise. You know, I specifically requested Dr. Raines assistance because of what you discovered."

"Because of what I found?" I dropped his hand like it was a hot charcoal.

"I'm sorry, Mr. Malone, you seem confused. I assumed Dr. Raines, Ted, told you why he was coming here."

Ted jumped in before I could respond. "I didn't let the cat out of the bag because I wanted to savor Matt's reaction on firm turf."

"Ahh … so you must be pleased with the results, Ted?" Dr. Russell said as he stood in front of us rubbing his hands together in a typical washing motion. Ted didn't answer. The doctor continued, "Well, now that everyone knows what this meeting is about, let's proceed to my lab, shall we?"

# CHAPTER 26

▼

Dr. Russell's finely polished black oxford shoes squeaked continuously as they glided him across the sterile, black and white checker-tiled lab floor; the irritating noise only disappeared when the doctor reached his destination at the far side of the room: a long narrow table. The lower portion of the table displayed four metal legs, the upper was hidden from view by a white sheet-like cloth, the same type I've seen many times before when viewing corpses at the morgue.

Ted and I joined Jim at the table immediately after he whisked the cover off the skeleton.

Small blue-colored tags were attached to various parts of the skeleton. I asked Dr. Russell why he needed so many tags for one skeleton. "All these tags represent the different parts of the body that helped me determine the sex, age, race, and injuries of the deceased. As soon as I complete my report, the tags will be disposed of."

The tag attached to the pelvic area intrigued me the most. I read it aloud. "Measurement of pelvic bones establishes person as male."

"Yes," Jim softly injected. "The difference in ratio between the length of pubes," he said pointing to the bottom back part of the pelvic region, "to Ischium," he slowly guided his hand to the bottom back part of the pelvic area, "is used for this purpose." He pulled his hand away from that spot and slipped it around the tag attached to the skull. "Now, the size of the skull also indicates whether the skeleton is male or female. A woman's is known to be significantly smaller." I was already aware of the differences in skull sizes between sexes due to my earlier visit to the Science Museum, but I let it slide.

Ted added more to the discussion. "You know, Jim is really fortunate to have the whole skeleton to work with."

"Oh, why is that?" I asked.

"Well," he replied, "sex is mistaken only ten-percent of the time when a complete skeleton is available, but when you just have a skull at your disposal, the rate of error increases to twenty-five percent."

I turned my attention back to Dr. Russell, now. "You said you could tell the age of a skeleton and if their were any injuries, too."

"That's correct," the coroner replied. "Just by using the naked eye alone, you can see that these bones are discolored and that some of the soil is still sticking to them." He ran his fingers up and down the side of the skeleton. "This information indicates to me that our skeleton wasn't someone recently deceased—he probably died around the end of the nineteenth century. And, the protuberance of this male's leg bone, here, is caused by horseback riding."

"Oh," I blurted out, "that means this guy could've been part of the Cox legacy after all."

The two doctors replied as one voice, "Afraid not, unless Mr. Cox has Native-American Indians for relatives."

"An Indian? What did you look at to determine the race, the cheekbones?"

"Go ahead, Ted," Jim said. "You're the expert."

"The shape of the skull, primarily." Ted ran his fingers gently along the outer edges of the skull. "If this guy were Caucasian, his skull would be narrower, the nose would project higher, the chin would be higher, and the cheekbones would be receding. Native American Indians have forward projecting cheekbones, and their dental features are different."

I ran my hand through my hair. "Wow! This skeleton info is not good news, then, is it?"

Both doctors shook their heads. Then Jim spoke, "Traditionally speaking, Indian tribes in the area have the right to request that the property be roped off and digging be discontinued. They'll need time to study the land and make a decision to whether it could be a sacred burial ground or not. It could mean the end to a much needed new school."

"Exactly," Ted replied.

"So what we need to do," Dr. Russell said in a very serious tone, "is determine, as soon as possible, what Indian Nation this skeleton came from. That's the reason Ted's been invited here. Once that's done, it'll be easier to prove whether the property was or wasn't an Indian burial ground."

"When you called me, Jim," Ted said, "you mentioned that the skeleton had something clutched in its hand. I'd like to see that item now, if I may."

"Certainly." Jim strolled over to a tall white cabinet that was pressed up against an outer wall, opened the top drawer, retrieved a couple items, and then returned to Ted and me. Now he carefully handed the first object off to the professor.

Ted removed his bifocals from his shirt pocket and perched them on the edge of his nose, before examining the item that was enclosed in a clear self-sealed bag. From where I was standing, it looked like Ted was holding a tiny piece of leather, medium-brown in color. "Not much to go on, is it?" Ted commented. "Could be from a medicine or parfleche bag. The parfleche bag was used to carry food and possessions. Did your crime scene investigator find anything else related to the skeleton?"

"Yes," the coroner replied, "two other things, but I don't know if they'll be any use to you either."

"You might as well let me look at them. You never can tell."

Jim gave Ted the next package and said, "I'm fairly certain this knife is what killed him: a direct blow to the heart."

Ted gazed at the knife for a couple minutes before letting us in on his thoughts. "Ah huh, this handy dandy item definitely wasn't created by an Indian. Settlers used this during hunting season ..."

Time to take a break from my friend's history lessons, I thought. I've got more pressing things to think about like the object that I placed in my pant pocket on the day I helped Ron move the skeleton out of the hole. My sixth sense was telling me that piece of pottery was probably the most important clue around—but what to do about it? "Say, if you don't mind, you two can continue your discussion without me. I need to examine your men's room—too much coffee this morning."

Jim waved me off. "Go ahead. We're not going anywhere. It's down the hall and to the left."

"Thanks." I left the lab and walked down the hall just far enough to be out of hearing range. Then I slipped my cell phone out of my suitcoat and dialed Mrs. Grimshaw's number. "Margaret, this is Matt. What? Oh, I'm in Anoka on business. Hey, did any of your diaries mention Indians? No? Nuts! Well, could you do me a favor? I'm short on time. Call my mother and ask her to find the shoebox that has my childhood mementoes in it. I'll explain later. Thanks."

# CHAPTER 27

▼

I told Mrs. Grimshaw to look for Indians,
And that's when I began to wonder what
I really knew about them.

Sure, many moons ago they roamed
Prairies, valleys, and mountain tops.
But they don't do that anymore.

Tepees, cliff dwellings, and earth lodges.
Buffalo hunts, birchbark canoes and totem poles.
Bows and arrows, spears and tomahawks.
Most of those were laid to rest long ago.

What was left of what I knew, then?
Tribes on reservations all across the land,
Designing blankets, pottery, jewelry and leather pieces.
Sharing peace pipes, vision quests, ceremonial dances …

It was eleven o'clock by the time Ted dropped me back at the Foley. I wanted to return sooner, but the professor insisted on stopping for brunch at a café near the U of M campus. Bad move. Several of his students were killing time there, in between classes, so they stopped by our table to talk shop. Dr. Raines, having a reputation for never turning people away, welcomed them with open arms.

Oh, well, I'm back on home turf now, and I'm going to make darn sure not a minute is wasted retrieving treasures from my childhood. With that in mind, I purposely decided to skip a trip to the fourth floor to check on Gracie and headed straight to the Foley's underground parking lot where the mud splattered Topaz was waiting for me. And yes, if you must know, the guy who parks in the slot next to me was over the line again for the umteenth time.

Since I couldn't get in on the driver's side, I disgustedly made my way to the passenger side, unlocked the door, opened the glove compartment and took out paper and a pen. Then in huge block letters I wrote: *Hey, fella, in case you haven't noticed, your parking slot hasn't been enlarged.* After I completed my message, I tucked it under the rude fellow's windshield wiper. Probably won't have any affect, but at least I vented. Now I returned to the open car door, closed the glove compartment, sat down on the passenger side, and slammed the door.

Of course, entering this side of the car didn't resolve anything. Damn! I still couldn't peel out of the parking lot because there was one more hurdle to jump— I needed to get my body over to the driver's side. Having been in this predicament many times before, I knew the movement from one seat to the other could be managed even though the space is rather tight.

When I finally returned to my apartment with my shoe box of memories, I found Gracie lying on a piece of paper that I assumed had been shoved under the door. Oh, crap! It was probably retaliation for the note I left earlier in the parking lot. I bent down, gently slipped my hand under the dog's furry front paws, pulled the paper from her body and stood again. Relief quickly flooded over me when I saw the flowery stationery. There was only one apartment dweller in this building that used such fancy paper: Margaret Grimshaw. Her beautifully scripted note requested that I come over to her place as soon as I arrived home. I chuckled. That was a little unrealistic. If I went straight over there, I'd come back to a smelly mess. One thing an animal owner learns in the early stages is that the animal's needs normally outweigh all others.

As soon as I arrived at Margaret's place, I began apologizing at once. "Sorry I couldn't get here any faster, but Gracie needed tending to."

My apartment neighbor remained firmly planted in her doorway, with her hands hidden behind her back. "Hush, Matt, there's no need to explain. I'm just thankful you found my note. I purposely left it on the little table in your hallway assuming you'd notice it there the quickest." So, she didn't slip it under the door as I thought. I suppose the breeze created by the door being closed was enough to lift the note off the table and float to the floor. On the other hand, it could've been Gracie's wild tail. Margaret drew her hands in front of her now, and my eyes quickly shifted from her face to them. They were covered with a white powdery substance.

As soon as she caught me staring at her hands, she said, "I've been keeping myself pretty busy while I waited for you to return." Now she waved me through her door like an usher does at a concert and added, "Come in. Please come in."

I sniffed the air as I entered her abode. "Where would you like me to sit? The living room or the kitchen?" I hoped the kitchen since the apartment reeked of freshly baked chocolate chip cookies. Yes, I had cookies this morning, but they were store bought—Margaret's are the real thing.

"Matt, you know how I'm always telling you that Italians like to celebrate with food?" I politely nodded. "Well, we'd better head for the kitchen then because we have something to celebrate."

I stepped behind my elderly neighbor and followed her to the next room. "Mind if I ask what we have to celebrate, Margaret? Neither of us is getting a job promotion or turning a year older."

She fluffed her rose-patterned apron, and some of the white stuff came off her hands. "Oh, this is much better than that. Ah, but first, would you be terribly upset to hear that I entered your living room while you were gone?" I shook my head in a negative manner. I knew Margaret wouldn't go into the other rooms of my apartment without good cause. Besides, I'm the one who gave her my spare key in the first place. "Good, because my intentions were just. When I put the note on the hall table, I noticed that the unread diaries were still sitting on the floor by your couch, waiting to be read, so I picked them up and brought them back here to finish the job for you."

No problem there—she just saved me some steps. "So we're celebrating because you found something useful in those diaries, then?"

My neighbor's wrinkled cheeks puffed up like a rooster about to crow. "I certainly did," she said as she rubbed her tiny hands together. "Why, I never dreamed sleuthing could be so much fun. Now I know exactly how Miss Marple felt when she was close to solving a case." She tapped my hands lightly. "I appreciate your asking this old woman to help."

Yes, but Miss Marple was only a fictional character that Agatha Christie created, I thought to myself, you're not. "Yeah, well, I needed the help," I muttered under my breath. She was getting too mushy on me. I hated that. I had to turn the tide. "Now about those diaries ..."

She frowned. "Young man, you need to learn patience—I'm getting to that. Here," she took a plate of cookies off her counter and set them on the table in front of me, "relax, have a few while I take care of the tea." She moved to the stove. As she started pouring water into her teapot she said in almost a whisper, "The very last diary held the clue you were looking for."

Too curious to be polite, I didn't wait to swallow what I had in my mouth. "What did it say?"

Mrs. Grimshaw brought the teapot to the table now. "Sorry, but I didn't understand what you asked. Perhaps you should practice manners along with patience. One is to swallow one's food before talking."

I took her grandmotherly advice and swallowed. "All right. Now what did the diary say?"

"It's not just what the diary said. After I finished reading all the books, I did some historical poking around, too. For instance, from 1873 to about 1894, the Catholic mission priest said mass once a month at Cedar Creek, and usually had dinner at one of the member's homes before riding back to his home parish in Anoka."

Not Anoka again, I thought to myself. "Hmm ... no. There was no mention of that in the diaries I read. So how does having dinner with a church member relate to Indians? I don't see the connection."

Margaret shared one of her honey smiles with me. "On a Sunday morning in January of 1883 light snow was already falling when the priest approached the mission church. So before mass started he mentioned to that month's host and hostess, neighbors of the Cox clan, that he didn't think it wise to stay for dinner with the possibility of a severe storm approaching, but they pressed him to stay. Well, at meal time, the priest finally shared the real reason he didn't want to remain in the territory. Earlier he had spotted a lone Indian riding through the woods on the path that leads back to his home parish. Of course, no one at the table seemed able to offer an explanation for an Indian to be in the area: Dakota Indians had been tossed out of Minnesota after the Sioux uprising in 1862, and the nearest group of Ojibwe were on the reservation in Mille Lacs."

"Mille Lacs?" I said as I hastened to Margaret's telephone that resided in the living room.

"Who are you calling?" Margaret asked from her kitchen table. "Rita?"

# CHAPTER 28

▼

I pressed my finger against my lips, said "Sh ...," and then I turned my back to Margaret so she couldn't hear my conversation. "Information desk please. Hi Joan, it's Matt Malone. I've got some work cut out for you. I need to know what type of weather central Minnesota was having in January of 1883." Joan asked if there was anything else I needed. "Nope, that will do it. Oh, I don't know when I'll be near my home phone, so just leave the info on my answering machine. Thanks." I hung up the phone and returned to Margaret who was just refreshing our cups of tea.

I could tell she was just dying to find out what my phone call was all about, but she didn't ask. She just placed the now empty teapot by her kitchen sink and sat back down. "You know Matt, you never did explain what my call to your mother was for this morning."

"You're right. I didn't." So before I sat at the table again, I pulled two objects from my front pant pocket. They were similar but, one was larger than the other. I placed them on the Thanksgiving-themed tablecloth in front of Margaret's tea-cup.

My neighbor's old eyes twinkled. "How interesting. But if we're going to have an art lesson, won't we need more pieces?"

"Sorry, that's all I have," I said as I leaned forward in my chair and pointed to the smaller piece of pottery. "When I was a wee lad, I found this piece on my uncle's family farm outside of Bismark, North Dakota. My uncle told me the Mandan Indians once roamed the area." I pointed to the other piece. "And this one, well, I pocketed it after I lifted the exposed skeleton from its burial site."

Margaret's barely visible eyebrows arched severely. "Let's see—you're impatient, lack manners, and you also steal stuff. I don't understand what makes you tick, Matt, but you should be ashamed of yourself." She adjusted her tri-focal glasses a bit before placing the pieces of pottery in her hands to study them more closely.

Hmm, I find it interesting that my mother and Margaret have now both told me they don't know what makes me tick, although my mom has also referred to me as a different *breed.* As I brushed my hand through my hair, Margaret's comments as well as my mother's vanished like water running down a sink. "Borrowed, not stolen," I stressed. "There's a huge difference."

"Humph, so you say. Well, the stolen slash borrowed one and yours sure look similar to me."

With Mrs. Grimshaw's hasty decision that the two pieces could be related, I stabbed my hand into my back pant pocket and brought forth a small book which I had found at the Minneapolis Public Library earlier today. "Ah huh." I handed the book to my neighbor. "Read page twenty-six. It's already marked."

She quickly flipped to the marked page. "Do I really have to read this? The print is so small. Oh, well, at least the pictures are a decent size. Let's see ... 'In the very early years of Mandan history, pottery was decorated with impressed cord. As Southern Mandan moved north, the two groups adopted each other's designs'." She placed the book on her table and examined the samples again. "My, oh my! The pieces here on the table look exactly like the pottery pictured in the book."

"I know," I said rather proud of my discovery. "And get this, the people called in to figure out which tribe the skeleton belongs to are on an entirely different wavelength. They think the Indian was Dakota because of the items the forensic team found at the site."

Margaret stayed silent for a moment before she spoke. "Are you planning to share this information with the police, Matt, or keep it to yourself?"

I combed my fingers through my hair. "I'm not exactly certain what and when I'll do anything at this point. All I know is that I'm not ready to divulge my secret to anyone outside of this room yet. My gut instincts tell me there's a lot more to the story than what's been brought to the surface." My hand jumped from my hair to my empty teacup and saucer. "What would bring a Mandan Indian to Minnesota? Cedar Creek sure doesn't run along the border of North Dakota. And why was he carrying objects only Dakota Indians use?"

The woman who was entertaining me didn't respond. Instead Margaret quietly shoved herself away from the table, without excusing herself. Must have a lot on her mind, I thought, because she always follows Miss Manners to the T. I turned in my chair to spy on her. When she reached her desk in the living room, she stopped, pulled her personal phone book from a drawer, opened it and began to dial. Who the heck was she calling, I wondered.

I tried to question her before she reached her party. "What …?"

Her only response was "Shh," as mischief shined in her eyes.

# CHAPTER 29

▼

We're drifting back to North Dakota,
past woods and rivers where the Sioux
and Mandan were first to camp and fish.

Settlers came next and greedily begged
soldiers to move the Indians from the land.
So tribes were resettled to sites called
reservations, and there the Nations remain.

The river banks now are but a distant memory for
Mandan and Sioux, who once fished in harmony. So too
the woods where they freely roamed; the forest has
been cleared to make way for farms, homes and factories.

It was strange how Mrs. Grimshaw and I came to the same conclusion at the exact same moment in time—that I would probably find the answers I was seeking if I drove to Bismark, North Dakota. And then my neighbor added, wouldn't it be nice if she, Margaret, kept me company on that long drive. Of course she'd stay clear of me once we arrived so I could do research. "There's an elderly friend I've been wanting to visit, so while you"re tracking down a professor who's knowledgeable in Indian culture, we can get caught up."

The journey from the cities to Bismark takes roughly seven hours or a full day so we left at the crack of dawn. As planned, Margaret brought plenty of snacks and refreshments to insure that I, the driver, wouldn't fall asleep at the wheel, which I appreciated greatly.

But now, as the last leg of our journey was about to commence, there was nothing left to munch on. My eyes and head were becoming heavier and heavier, and all I wanted to do was take a long snooze. Luckily, my neighbor, without realizing it, saved the Topaz and us from extinction when she jolted me awake with, "Matt, did you see it?"

"Wha? Huh? See what?" I asked as I rubbed my gritty eyes with my one free hand.

"Bismark's sign, of course, welcoming us to their fair city."

"No, I didn't." I cleared my throat. "Must've been too hypnotized by the road. That's what happens when there's too long a stretch with nothing to look at. Well, at least one of us was alert enough to notice." Amazingly, the tension in my rigid body vanished with the news that our destination was nearly in front of us. I turned towards Margaret to see how she was faring. From what I could see, it appeared she survived the trip better than me. Maybe because she wasn't behind the steering wheel.

Mrs. Grimshaw stopped staring out the window and met my eyes. "Can you believe Thanksgiving is in two days, Matt?"

"Nope."

"Maybe I can convince my friend to let me prepare a nice dinner for the three of us. How would you feel about that?"

I yawned. "Anything's better than eating by ourselves at some stupid truck stop."

"Great! I'll see what I can do," she said as she began tucking her crochet project back into her flimsy plastic bag obtained from our local drugstore. "Oh, dear. I just thought about Rita. Did you have a chance to tell her that you wouldn't be spending Thanksgiving with her?"

"No need to."

"What? I can't believe you'd be that insensitive. Mister, if you don't want to lose that wonderful girlfriend of yours, you'd better get on that cell phone as soon as you drop me off. Do you understand?"

I winked and saluted her. "Yes, Margaret. But she won't be home."

"Well, then call her at work. I'm sure you have that number engraved on your brain."

"She won't be there either," I laughed. I was enjoying the little game I was playing with Margaret since she's always fooling with my head.

"And why not?"

"Because she isn't in Minnesota. She and her parents drove out of town to visit an ailing relative. And incidently, just for the record, before she left she called and cancelled our plans."

My neighbor's eyes almost popped out of their sockets. "For heaven's sake! Why didn't you say that in the first place, instead of setting me up to be defensive, hmm?"

"Because, dear lady, for far too long you've gotten away with all that teasing you do to me, so I felt this was the perfect opportunity to pay you back."

My petite passenger permitted her childish giggle to fill the air while she buttoned her coat and slipped her leather gloves on. We were only ten minutes from her friend's place now. "So where did Rita and her folks have to drive to?" she inquired.

"Bismark. Isn't that insane?"

"You're teasing me again, right?"

"Nope." I brushed my hand through my hair. "I'm being totally honest this time." "I suppose you'll call her later then?"

I caught a glimpse of a street sign hanging over the interstate now. We were drawing near the apartment building where Margaret's longtime friend lived. I quickly switched over to the right lane and took the next exit ramp off the freeway. "Yeah, I'll try to reach her on her cell phone. Hopefully she has it with her." I stopped at the top of the ramp, and then when it was clear to go I made a sharp left turn. Once I rounded the corner of White and Deephaven, I guided the Topaz into the huge parking lot for Capitol Apartments.

Since the parking area was so large, I assumed there were several units located here, but there was only one, and it was designated for seniors only. I felt a twinge of guilt run through me when I thought about Margaret being dropped off in the middle of nowhere and my not knowing a thing about her supposed friend. Well, that's not quite true. I had been told that the person moved out of the Foley a month before I arrived.

It really bugged me that my neighbor was being so closed mouthed about her friend. Usually she wants to share all. Was her friend a man or a woman, I wondered. If the person was a man, could she possibly have been in love with him at one time?

I parked the car and turned the engine off. Margaret instinctively began to open her door. "Hey, despite what you think, I do have some virtues. Like, I usually help my lady friends out of the car, so just relax." I went to the back of the car, retrieved my neighbor's luggage, and then made my way to the passenger side of the car and opened the door. As soon as Margaret stepped out she reached for her small overnight bag. "Put that down, woman," I said. "Chivalry isn't dead yet. I planned to carry that to the lobby for you."

"No you're not!" my neighbor said in a strong high-pitched tone. "You need to get to your hotel and check in before it's too late." I stole a look at my wristwatch. She was right. I hadn't used a charge card to reserve my room, and it was definitely past the time I was supposed to show. Since her bag was rather light, I gave in. "All right, take your bag, but are you certain your friend is waiting for you?"

She began yawning and covered her mouth with her gloved hand. "I'm positive."

"I feel like I'm forgetting something. Let's see, you already gave me your friend's phone number, right?"

"Yes, Matt."

"Okay, I'll call you sometime tomorrow and discuss Thanksgiving." I went back to the driver side of the car and watched as Margaret disappeared into the building. Once the door closed behind her, I waited three minutes more before driving off just in case she came back out.

# CHAPTER 30

▼

After I got a room for the night at the Super 8 Motel on Capitol Avenue, I decided to swing by the University of Mary, a distance of 5.5 miles from there, to see if the main office was still open for the day. If it was, I planned to ask which professor might be more beneficial for me to speak with—the instructor for North Dakota History or Indian Studies. Knowing that could save me considerable time tomorrow morning.

When I arrived on campus, the Admission's Office door was ajar and several people were still milling about. The person I immediately zoned in on was this fifty-something waif of a woman sitting behind a huge oak desk that held a plaque reading *Office Administrator*. I strolled directly to her desk and introduced myself. "Hi, Matt Malone." I flashed my PI card in front of her face. "Sorry to barge in on you so late in the day, but I just got into town and really need your assistance."

The female with curly coal-black hair eagerly exposed her pearly whites while she swiftly shoved her paperwork aside that she'd been working on when I arrived. "Tell me, Mr. Malone," she asaid in a syrupy tone, "Where exactly did you drive in from?"

"The Twin Cities."

"Yeah, that's an incredibly long haul. My youngest sister lives down there," she informed him as she stuck her well-manicured hand out now and reached across her desk. "Nice to meet you. I'm Marsha. So what kind of help do you need? I'm not allowed to give out any confidential information," she winked, "even to a good-looking PI like you."

As I waited for sly undertones to come from others in the room, the heat along my collar area slowly rose to my face. Luckily, none came. "No problem, Marsha. What I need from you is strictly considered public knowledge."

"Oh! Okay, let's hear it."

"One of the cases I happen to be working on pertains to an Indian skeleton: possibly Mandan. So, which of your professors would be better suited to discuss that tribe with me, the one teaching North Dakota History or Indian Studies?"

She picked up the Bic pen that was resting against her right hand and began examining it. "Actually, here at our university, both those classes are taught by the same person, Professor Kathleen Gibson, but she won't be any help to you."

Surprised by her candor, I asked, "And why not?"

"Her two classes are held only on Mondays, so she left for the holiday already: her parents' place in Tampa, Florida."

"Damn," I said under my breath as I ran my hand through my hair. Louder I added, "Is there anyone else you can think of who might be able to help me?"

"Well," she licked her bright-red lips, "there's an old Indian woman living on the other side of town who happens to be part Mandan. She's been a guest speaker for Professor Gibson's classes many times. She's very knowledgeable in tribal history and a wonderful story-teller.

I had come this far. I guess it didn't matter who I talked to as long as they knew what they were talking about. "Do you mind writing her number and address down?"

"Of course not." She flashed me a wide grin then spun towards her card file, flipped through it, and quickly copied the information I'd asked for. When she was finished, she pulled the sticky note off the pad and handed the slip of paper to me. "Here you go, Mr. Malone. I hope she can be of help."

A serious tone suddenly overcame me, "Thanks, so do I." Then I did an about face and walked out the door.

# CHAPTER 31

▼

My stomach was growing impatient with me as I left the Administration Build-ing behind. It was supper time and when you get in a set routine the stomach offers no reprieve if you're a second late with the chow. Too bad. I didn't have time at this juncture to respond to its complaints. I had more pressing things to attend to, like going straight back to my motel room and gathering my thoughts before calling the Indian woman.

Now that I was back at the motel room and sat at the desk where the phone was, I twiddled with the phone cord and wondered how Rose Running Water Jenson would react to my call. Would she be helpful to a PI or not? Well, I'd soon find out. Her phone stopped ringing, and someone was about to speak "Hello."

"Er, hello. Is this Rose Jenson?"

"Yes, it is," the soft but firm elderly voice replied.

"My name is Matt Malone. A secretary at the University of Mary gave me your number just a few minutes ago. I hope I'm not disrupting your supper hour?"

"You're not," she said with a pleasant tone in her voice, "It's perfectly fine to call at this hour. We won't be sitting down for sometime yet. So would I be cor-rect in assuming this call pertains to the Mandan Indians?"

My foot was in the door now, and I just needed to get the rest of my body in. "Yes, but before I go into any great detail, I'd like to be up front with you—tell you what I do for a living."

She sighed. "If you think you must."

"I'm a private investigator."

"Move along, young man. I mean continue."

Whew! I swept my hand through my wind-blown hair. For a minute there, I thought that was the end of our phone conversation. "My small business is run out of the Twin Cities. However, sometimes I find myself traveling to other parts of the country in order to finish what I've been hired to do. Such is the case in this situation. The information I need can only be acquired from someone living in this area."

"I see," she said politely.

"I drove to Bismark, today, hoping to speak with a college professor who is knowledgeable in the ways of this region's Indians to learn what I could about the Mandan people and their art. The mistake I made was in assuming there would be more than one professor to speak with."

"No, just Dr. Gibson."

I tugged at the phone cord trying to straighten out the mess I had made. "So I was informed, and I missed her—she's already left on vacation."

"Voices tend to say a lot, Mr. Malone. I've listened to your's very carefully," she said. "It shows determination, and I like the fact that you are a seeker of truth. In my world that is always a good sign. Be at my home by eight tonight. Good-bye." The phone went dead.

I placed the handset back in the cradle. "That's it?" I thought I'd be interrogated to the ninth degree, especially when I mentioned that I was a PI. What a generous woman. I wonder if she opens her home to any stranger who calls. "I must arrive with a gift, but what?" I snapped my fingers. "Sweets! Yeah, that'll do." Who ever passes up goodies? Just as the food word passed my lips, my stomach began the churning process again. I patted my rotund tummy to soothe it. "Don't worry. Food's a comin' just as soon as I can figure out where to get it."

▼

# CHAPTER 32

Hotels and motels always provide a restaurant directory in each guest room; it takes the backseat only to the Gideon Bible. It's usually found sitting next to the phone, and true to form, the availability and placement of this room's directory was no exception. "Hmm? Kentucky Fried Chicken or Perkins? Having spent too many hours in the car already, I felt I could use some muscle action. Perkins, which was within walking distance, also offered plenty of sweets, and it had a wider assortment of meals.

When I finished my three-course meal at Perkins which included Caesar Salad, onion soup, and a burger, I took my to-go order and meandered back to the Super 8 office where I inquired about Rose Jenson's address. "Oh," the teen-aged-looking, pocked-marked thirty-ish male clerk said, "Valley was renamed not too long ago. What you really want is Deephaven. Maybe you noticed a newer apartment building when you first entered town?"

"That wouldn't be Capitol Apartments, would it?" I asked.

"Yeah, that's the one."

"Thanks," I said as I started to exit. "I know exactly where that's at." Heck, I'd dropped Mrs. Grimshaw off there only a couple hours ago.

Perhaps I should call her before I go over there just to make certain she's okay. She wasn't expecting to hear from me till tomorrow—but what if things didn't pan out the way she wanted them to? On the other hand, if she's visiting a man friend, she may not appreciate the intrusion even if she's in her nineties. I opted not to call. Mrs. Grimshaw didn't need some stupid PI mucking up her privacy.

With Daylight Savings Time fully in motion now, the parking lot at Capitol Apartments had taken on an eerie quality—like someone had dropped a black drop cloth from the sky. At least no snow nor rain had been added to the mix to make it seem more offbeat.

There was one parking spot left at the furthest edge from the building, and I took it. I shut the motor off, stepped out of the Topaz, and then led my body footstep by footstep to the apartment's main entrance over which hung one forty-watt bulb. Either the hospital in town was very busy mending residents from these digs, or the tenants never ventured out after dark. Granted, it is a new building, but how new is new? If I lived here, the owners would be so deluged with complaints from me that the lighting situation would be remedied pronto.

I buzzed Rose Jenson's apartment number and waited. "Yes?" a hollow microphone voice responded.

I leaned against the entrance lobby speaker so I wouldn't have to shout. "This is Matt Malone. You're eight o'clock appointment."

"Just a minute, please."

I heard a familiar noise, and then the locked inner lobby door magically came unlocked. A vacant and waiting elevator was two steps from the door so I hastily stepped in before someone else pressed for its service on another floor. The elevator was much roomier than the one at the Foley. I pressed the button for the second floor, and the door closed.

When the elevator door slid open, Ms. Jenson was there to greet me. I quickly noted her dimensions and realized she and Mrs. Grimshaw could pass for sisters—even though one was of North American Indian descent and the other of Italian. Each had a small thin frame but was not frail in any respect and, they were both approximately ninety years of age. The years had been good to Rose. Wrinkles on her face were hardly visible and I was pretty certain it wasn't due to the makeup she used. There didn't appear to be signs of any.

We shook hands as soon as I got off the elevator, and then Rose asked me to follow her down the hall. I liked the width of the hallway here, more space to maneuver your body if you met someone coming down the hall. The passageways at my apartment complex only allow for shoulder to shoulder combat. That's all right if you're the lovey-dovey type with everyone you meet. I'm not.

The elderly Indian woman stopped in front of the door marked 204, opened it wide, and ushered me in. The warmth of the living room along with the soft glow coming from her antiquities made me receptive to the journey back in time; so many objects and paintings from Rose's heritage. I recognized a few pieces from books I had perused or museums visited, but many I'd never seen. "Such beautiful history you've surrounded yourself with," is all I managed to say.

Rose's eyes shined as she gazed at the space she was welcoming me into. "Why, thank you."

Funny, there was a hint of lavender in the air. Mrs. Grimshaw, my neighbor, likes that scent too. Maybe it was popular in their youth. Although, from what I've seen on TV commercials the last couple of years, it's become a very popular fragrance for essential oils and lotions. Helps you relax, supposedly. I must say it seemed to be working on me. I was very nervous about this meeting when I pulled in the parking lot. Now I was as calm as a turtle.

"Have a seat, Mr. Malone," the Indian woman said pointing to an ancient hand-carved rocker.

"Before I do, let me thank you again for helping me out." I released the box of brownies I had purchased at Perkins, into her care, and then I placed my hands on the back of the rocking chair and examined it. "Are you sure you want me to sit in this?" I asked. "I don't think it can handle my weight."

Rose put her free hand to her lips. "Of course it can. Many men before you have sat in it. It is made from a strong tree."

I sat. "By the way, you can drop the Mr. Malone. Just call me Matt."

"Well, then, Matt it is." She stared at me for a moment. "My, my, it looks as though the chair was meant for you."

"It's very comfortable."

"Now, is there anything I can get you before we begin? A glass of water, tea, or perhaps coffee?"

I wrapped my hands around the arms of the old rocker. It felt good. "If it's not too much trouble, a cup of coffee would be nice."

Rose raised her soft voice a notch, "Coffee it is." Then she sat down on her buffalo-print-covered couch and waited patiently.

How was the coffee going to get into the living room if the hostess was not setting foot in the kitchen, I wondered. Usually one goes to get it unless you have a maid, and I hadn't seen or heard another person in Rose's dwelling since I'd arrived. I decided to chalk it up to one of life's mysteries and didn't ask. Instead, I relaxed my back into the groove of the rocker and began rocking.

About two minutes into the wait, the sound of a tea kettle whistling traveled from the kitchen to us. Hmm, maybe Rose's husband or other family member is preparing the libations. A moment later, I heard dishes rattling, silverware clinking, and finally someone approaching. The person treaded lightly. It definitely wasn't a man. There would be a lot more noise. Unfortunately, the back of the rocker hid the newcomer from me, but Rose had an excellent view of the area leading up to where we sat, and now she shared a pleasant smile.

# CHAPTER 33

▼

"Thank you. Just set it there," Rose commanded firmly, "in front of him."

I shifted my gaze from Rose and focused it squarely on the person who was now placing a tray on the narrow birch coffee table. Even though the new arrival, a woman, was stooped over and her back was to me, I knew instantly who she was. Of course, I was in denial. I kept telling myself I was imaging things—heck a lot of people look the same from behind.

All it took was her familiar voice to confirm what I believed to be true. "Look at that. You brought brownies to go with the coffee. See Rose. I told you what a nice young man he can be. If only he could resolve those other vices he has."

Mrs. Grimshaw was embarrassing the heck out of me, and I began to wonder why I even came to Ms. Jenson's apartment tonight. I wanted to defend myself, but nothing tumbled out.

"What's wrong, Matt?" Margaret pressed. "You look like you swallowed the canary and the cat chasing it."

"It's just ..."

"Yes?" my neighbor inquired.

"It's just that your presence surprised me. I mean, sure I dropped you here a couple hours ago, but I never imagined you'd be spending time with the one person I needed to speak with."

"Everyone has secrets, Matt, and I'm no exception. Besides, I figured if you failed in your research at the college, you'd be delighted to learn I had a backup plan for you. As she straightened her small back, she tapped one lone finger to her chin. "I find it very strange, you a PI, didn't recognize the phone number the college people gave you."

I shifted my eyes to Rose and then to Margaret again. "I swear, Mrs. Grimshaw, you're trying to sign on as my permanent assistant, aren't you?"

"That's not such a bad idea," she said sternly, "considering you completely missed the phone number connection."

"Okay, okay. I admit I missed it, but I've got an explanation." Before I explained though, I reminded myself to stay calm so as not to scare the hostess. "I had other more pressing things on my mind at the time you presented me with your friend's number, so I never got around to seeing what you had written down. Eventually, the slip of paper you gave me got shoved into my wallet, and there it's remained." I glanced at the two-tone blend of brown carpet my shoes were resting on. "Being a private eye isn't just about driving somewhere to do a bit of light research. There's plenty of dangerous scenario that's crossed my path that you know absolutely nothing about."

Rose acted like she had heard enough. She pushed herself off the couch, walked to a side table, picked up a lose eagle feather, and then she returned and stood between the two of us. "I wish only peace in my home, please. Come, Margaret, sit beside me before you get yourself too fired up."

Rose's petite Italian visitor shutdown and quietly joined her on the couch.

As soon as they sat, Rose patted her friend's loose hand, the one that rested between them. "There dear, calmness is always better than being all knotted up inside." Margaret shut her eyes as Rose continued, "I hate to see one of your vices of old become active again." She winked at me.

So Rose thought Mrs. Grimshaw's weakness of getting too wired was stashed away long ago. Too bad I knew differently. It's nice to see that things we were taught in Catholic school still apply—like in the great scheme of things, no one escapes imperfection, except God.

A few minutes later, my neighbor opened her eyes and began conversing with her friend in a child-like whisper. "I'm truly sorry if I've upset you Rose. I didn't mean to. For some reason I can't explain, I get a kick out of giving Matt a hard time. Perhaps it relates back to my never having children to fret over."

Rose squeezed her hand then looked in my direction. "Matt, Margaret filled me in on some of what's been gong on, so I feel it's only fair that I present my background to you now. I am part Mandan and part Hidasta, Mandan being the stronger in me. At one time, the Mandan people lived in the central area of North Dakota and were 9,000 strong. You probably already know about the smallpox epidemic of 1837 and how it just about obliterated my people. Anyway, ten years later, with so few Mandan survivors, a decision was made to join the Hidasta tribe, resulting in a much stronger Siouan Nation."

Margaret leaned towards the coffee table in order to reach her coffee cup. "So, Rose, is it remotely possible that the skeleton Matt helped uncover is Mandan?"

Our hostess opened the box of brownies that I brought and passed them to Margaret who passed them unto me. "Depends," she said. "I need to see what your neighbor found before I can draw any conclusion. Did you happen to bring the fragment of pottery you discovered, Mr. Malone, I mean Matt?"

"I did. I figured whichever professor I spoke with would want to examine it." I popped a bit more brownie in my mouth before I pulled a tiny kleenex wrapped object out of my winter jacket, which hung over the back of the rocker, and placed it on the table in front of Rose. "Well, what do you think?"

The Indian woman took the article from the table and cradled it in her hand as if it were a newborn. A hush fell over the room—it felt too sacred a moment to speak. Rose's dark eyes longingly traced the pattern set into the pottery by her ancestors. "Yes!" her voice said with enthusiasm. "This was definitely created by the Mandan not the Hidasta. Clay work created by the Hidasta before the union was check-stamped."

I drew in a deep breath and then released it. "All Right! But that still doesn't explain why a Mandan ventured so far from home and why he was carrying objects from other Sioux tribes."

Margaret put her cup down on the table. "Rose, did your elders ever tell you if the Sioux and Mandan traveled together?"

I cheered Margaret on,"Good point."

Rose answered sleepily, "The stories that have been passed down to me only mention the Sioux mingling with the Mandan, nothing about travel." She yawned. "I don't know if you've had time to read up on the Sioux yet, but they were a seasonal people who frequently found themselves sharing common area with other long-term residents."

I took another bite of brownie, washed it down with lukewarm coffee, and then said, "I've actually had the privilege of seeing the skeleton up close twice, but not being an expert on Indians, I have no clear cut way of distinguishing one tribe from another. Perhaps you could enlighten me, Rose. For example, give me more detailed bone structure differences."

The Indian woman closed her eyes as if she was drawing from her memory. At least I hoped that's what she was doing and not going to sleep. "A Mandan's nose is narrow, straight and shorter than the Sioux's. The nose of a Sioux is arched." Her eyes snapped open suddenly, and she placed her aging hand on the outside upper half of her face. "And their cheekbones are higher than ours."

I reached in my shirt pocket to retrieve a small notepad and pen, and then started writing. "When the two different tribes shared the same camp area, were the young women allowed to mix with males of the opposite tribe?"

"Of course," Rose replied, "but it was frowned upon much as the marriage of a Catholic and a Lutheran was many, many years ago."

As I slipped the pen and notebook back in my pocket, I caught a glimpse of my watch: ten o'clock. Time to return to the motel and get some much needed shut-eye. "Well, ladies I believe it's time for me to hit the road."

"You don't need to go yet, Mr. Malone," Rose stated. "I'm sure you have more questions."

I patted my knees. "They can wait. When I spoke with you earlier, I told you I wouldn't waste your whole evening, and I meant it." I pushed my weary body out of the rocker and watched for a while as the chair nodded back and forth. "Thanks again for seeing me on such short notice, Rose." I extended my hand to her as I did when we first met earlier. Then I turned to my neighbor, and said, "Good-night, Margaret."

"Good-night, Matt."

Rose slipped her tiny frame off the couch and stood next to me.

"If you think of anything else that would be helpful to me, Rose, save it for tomorrow."

"All right." Now the Indian woman stepped in front of me and led me to the door. "Sometimes," she said, "when I sleep on it, memories come flooding back." With that she turned the knob and opened the door. "Maybe tonight will be one of those nights, Matt."

Already struggling with a yawn that was trying to get out, I somehow managed the words, "Let's hope so." I wished Rose good-night and headed to the elevator alone.

# CHAPTER 34

▼

When I stepped into my dark motel room twenty minutes later, I noticed a tiny red glow coming from the table that sat by the TV. Of course, my mind was too darn fried to realize what might be creating the effect. All that ran through my head, at that precise moment, was to find the main light source as soon as possible.

My fingers heard the message loud and clear. They immediately zipped up and down the wall searching for the light switch I remembered seeing only a couple hours earlier. In three seconds they found what they were looking for. I flicked the light on and strolled over to the table. Ah, the phone was the culprit. Someone had left a message, but who? I hadn't spoken to Rita or my family yet. I quickly pressed the message retrieve button.

"Matt, this is Rose Jenson." I rubbed my head. I just left her. What could she possibly have to share that just couldn't wait? "After you departed, Margaret and I got to discussing our Thanksgiving menu." Oh, yes, Margaret was going to ask her about having our Thanksgiving meal with her. "That's when I realized I didn't tell you to plan on joining us for dinner. I thought if we eat at noon you and Margaret can start back to the cities at a reasonable time. If that doesn't work for you, just tell me tomorrow when we see each other again."

I deleted the message, and then I went to the sink to get a glass of water, came back and turned on the TV. For some reason I wasn't quite ready for sleep yet even though my body told me otherwise.

While I stood watching the news, I pulled the orange blossom decorated bedspread off the bed and got undressed. My clothes got relegated to the double bed that I didn't plan to lay claim to.

The weather guy on the local news channel declared a chance of a snowstorm during the night depending, of course, on which direction the wind blew. Just what Margaret and I needed, I thought, to get stuck in Bismark a couple extra days. Hey, hold it there, Matt. That meant Rita and her folks would also be stranded here. Now that was a nice thought. Really lovely!

Hmm, I wonder what the luscious Miss Sinclair is doing right this minute? Well, find out. I padded over to the coat rack where my jacket was hanging and pulled my cell phone from one of the pockets. Now I promptly punched the code for selecting a saved number and requested that Rita's be dialed.

Her phone only rang twice before a sleepy voice responded, "Hello, this is Rita Sinclair."

"Surprise!" I said using a medium-volume voice.

"Matt? Is that really you? Or am I just dreaming?"

"Nope, Rita, you're not dreaming. The knight of your dreams is really calling you. I didn't wake you did I?"

She cleared her throat. "Actually, you timed your call perfectly. I just slipped under the bedcovers."

"Hmm, now that's something I'd love to see."

Rita teased in her sultry voice, "Why, Mr. Malone, you shock me."

"Nothing new, right? Hey, how's your uncle doing?" I sipped some water from my glass. "Do you think he'll make it through the holidays?"

"He's in stable condition right now—but he could take a turn for the worse at any time. Mom and Dad are spending as much time at the hospital as they can. I stay behind sometimes to help get things done around here."

"I'm sure your aunt appreciates that," I said.

"Tell me—how did your day at the office go? Any new cases brewing?"

I was tired of standing so I sat on the edge of the bed. "You're going to love this ..."

"What?" Rita eagerly asked. "Come on, Matt, I'm waiting."

I cut the TV noise in half because it was disturbing my conversation, and I also didn't want Rita finding out where I was before I announced it. "I wasn't at the office today."

"Oh, you worked from home then?"

"Nope."

She giggled. "You're sure not making this easy. You and Gracie goofed off instead?"

I laughed too. "Not quite. Gracie's spending a few days with my parents."

Rita's tone got serious rather fast. "Matt, you're all right, aren't you?"

"Yes, yes," I said for emphasis. "Mrs. Grimshaw and I just went on a little road trip to gather information for a case I'm working on. We ended up in a wonderful old town."

"Oh," my girlfriend sounded disappointed. "I wish it could've been me sitting next to you in that old beat up Topaz."

I sure was thankful Rita couldn't see my face when the next words flowed from my mouth. "Well, don't fret, Honey. We'll take a nice ride together very soon."

"Mr. Malone, who are you kidding? You know that's not true. I'll be up here several more days, and then it's back to the old grindstone."

"Ah, but Miss Sinclair, you forget your man in shining armor can take care of anything, and he has it all planned out for you."

"You do? Well, lay it out for me."

"Most certainly," I said. "Just give me your aunt's address, and my trusty stead and I will be there in a flash." I snapped my fingers.

"Matt," Rita whined, "I'm too tired for this type of joking. Besides I know your true identity, and you're not Sir Lancelot."

"Darn. I thought I was. Okay, Rita, you win. I'll just return to my tale about where Margaret and I drove today."

She yawned into the phone, "Yes, please do. You never said where you two ended up and I think it would be a nice change to hear about reality."

I repositioned my body on the bed before I continued. "Well, remember the part where I said you're going to love this?"

"Yes," she said drawing her reply out.

"Margaret and I happen to be in Bismark."

My girlfriend's, "What?" almost busted my eardrum. "Put Mrs. Grimshaw on the phone, right now. I want her to verify what you just said."

"No can do," I replied. "She's staying with an old friend, and I just came from there a few minutes ago. You'll just have to trust me on this one, sweetheart, if you really want to see me. Now the weatherman has been saying that we may be socked in with snow tomorrow, so I was thinking we should probably hit the bar scene tonight, that is if you're not too tired."

No answer came immediately, but it finally came. "All right, you can have my aunt's address Mr. Malone, but you'd better have a darn good map of Bismark because if you don't show up, you and I are history."

Now that's what I call one trusting gal.

# CHAPTER 35

▼

The radio alarm shook me from my sleep at seven-thirty a.m. sharp. I wasn't quite ready to admit that a new day had dawned, so I stayed in my reclining position for a wee bit longer and reflected on the hours I had spent with my girlfriend the night before. It had been a good month since Rita and I had done anything together. The Heritage Festival at St. Anthony on the Main seemed like eons ago. I was so content just hanging out with my lady friend that I didn't even mind the fact she beat me two out of three games of pool; there was a table at the back of Charlie's Bar where we finished off the night. Naturally the loser had to buy the winner a drink. Pretty cheap evening. Rita doesn't like the fancy-smancy fruity drinks that most other women do; she prefers a cold beer on tap.

I finally sat up and absorbed my surroundings. Motel rooms suck—but if you need a place to drop your body when far from home they suffice.

My eyes finally rested on the curtains keeping the morning out. I noticed that the fuzzy floral floor-length drapes covering the window in the room didn't quite match up. Because of this misfit I was treated to a six inch view of the world outside whether I wanted to see it or not. I didn't like the show. It was rather depressing; snow coming down like I hadn't seen since I was a kid.

This was one time I definitely didn't need my sixth sense to warn me of impending danger. My eyes were doing a fine job of filtering the mess out there and sending it on to my brain. I slowly rose and walked to the window. The cars in the parking lot were already covered with about four inches of snow. I turned from the window and padded over to the table where I had left the remote control for the TV set and began surfing for a local channel. Once I found one, I sat on the bed and glued my eyes to the set. Well, there wasn't much else to do.

The weather played the main role in the newsroom this morning. I imagine this is the most excitement they ever get up in Bismark. Anyway, the young news reporter was strutting his opening line which would immediately bring the follow-up commentary from the weatherman. "So Bruce, how much snow do you think we'll actually get? I'm anxious to get my snowmobile out and take it for a ride."

The fellow with the dark mane of hair shook his head. "Well, Randy, I'd say this looks like one of the worst storms we've had in a long time. I'm going to go out on a limb and say another four inches at least. Then it should start to taper off around midnight, just in time for the onslaught of Thanksgiving traffic." His face shined like a Christmas tree.

With nothing better to do with my time I mostly watched the boob tube the rest of the day—with only short breaks in between. I took one trip to the bathroom to take care of my bathing needs and the other to make darn sure I got my free continental breakfast.

I was thankful that there was a hallway that led to the breakfast nook area from our rooms our rooms or I would've probably skipped breakfast. Then again, maybe not because I stocked up enough food to make my breakfast equivalent to two meals since I knew I wouldn't be going anywhere for lunch. I loaded a tray with two juices, a banana, an apple, two styrofoam cups of coffee, a couple jelly rolls, some toast and of course a bowl of oatmeal. I felt like a bear getting ready for hibernation as I headed back to my cave, room. Yes, it was storming outside all right, but inside I was nice and cozy just thinking about the business and pleasure I completed before the storm hit.

# CHAPTER 36

▼

Mrs. Grimshaw called me right before eight to let me know our Thanksgiving plans were still on schedule for today. "Hooray! We're in business," she clucked wildly. "The turkey's in the oven, and the roads are being plowed. Now just don't be late, Matt."

"I'll be on time," is all I replied sleepily. What I wanted to say but didn't was how surprised I was that two very elderly women were able to get a huge meal for three whipped together, especially since no one in Bismark was able to get to any grocery store yesterday. A reply was forthcoming anyway, as if Margaret knew what I was thinking. Apparently the two of them went to the store not long after I dropped her off; Rose had listened to the weather reports all morning and decided she'd take them seriously.

"By the way, I told Rose how you much you love all that traditional Thanksgiving food so be prepared for a full blown meal. There will be no skimping on our watch. We're from the old school you know. Tee hee," she giggled.

No skimping. I patted my stomach. Now that's the kind of cooking I liked.

As I set the phone down in its cradle, my nose caught a whiff of something very familiar. You may think this is crazy, but my senses were so heightened by the mere anticipation of a nice Thanksgiving meal that I actually thought I smelled turkey and pumpkin pie.

I shook my head to clear my nostrils. Enough of that nonsense, Malone. What you really should be concerned about is what the new day is offering.

I hadn't dressed yet so of course I peeked outside through the same small opening in the curtains that was provided to me yesterday. Wow, things had changed drastically overnight. The sun was shining brightly, and mounds of glistening snow, created by a snowplow while I slept, stared back at me daring me to make them move from their new home against the curbing edge. How the heck did the Topaz fare, I wondered.

My eyes scanned the lumps of cars in the motel parking lot until they spotted the one that was shaped like the style of mine. Not too bad. The Topaz was covered with snow from front to back—except where the windows were. Some kind person removed the snow from all six windows, perhaps the manager. If so, it was a nice gesture considering I was staying at a low-priced motel.

No scraping of windows, but I still needed to remove the remaining blanket of snow off the rest of the car. Lucky me, ever since I've gotten caught in a few hairy situations, weather—wise, I've made darn sure my trunk is loaded with the following: container of sand, sleeping bag, shovel, whisk broom, candle and food rations.

I backed away from the curtains. Okay, after I shower and shave, I'll get dressed and clean the snow off the car. Then I'll see what's left at the breakfast spread. If everyone ate like I did yesterday, the cupboard is probably already bare.

Before checking out of the motel for good, I thanked the balding middle-aged manager for cleaning off my car windows.

"Sorry, it wasn't me, Mister Malone. Must've been one of the early risers."

"Oh, well, whoever did it—it was a nice surprise to discover that I didn't need to scrape my windows." I took my receipt from him and added, "Have a nice Thanksgiving," and headed for the door.

"Thanks," the manager replied. "You too."

Not knowing how well or quickly the local roads get cleared around these parts after a snowstorm, I purposely allowed myself a few extra minutes to get to Rose's apartment. Heck, after being warned about my arrival for the festivities, I didn't want to find out what it was like to sit down to eat with two angry nonagenarians—riding home with one would be bad enough.

I buzzed Rose's apartment number and patiently waited for her to release the lock on the inner lobby door. Since I already knew my way to her apartment, no one greeted me as I stepped off the elevator this time. I had only walked a few steps down the wide hallway when I saw Margaret standing in an open doorway. I immediately saluted her, and she shot a salute back to me.

As soon as I reached my neighbor I gave her a quick hug. "Gosh, I feel like I'm standing on the fourth floor of the Foley, right outside your apartment."

"Well, I hate to break it you, but you're not."

I ran my cool hand through my hair. "I know, but the hall is filled with the same rich aromas that I've grown accustomed to coming from your place." I licked my lips now.

Margaret looked at me sharply. "Don't start salivating yet, Matt. Wait till you see what we've prepared."

I raised my hand as if I was taking an oath. "I'll try." I walked through the door and went straight to the living room. "Where's Rose?" I asked.

My neighbor took my coat, and then she removed the long chef apron her friend had loaned her and placed both items on an arm of the couch. "In the kitchen carving the turkey."

"Would you like some help, Rose?" I questioned in a much louder voice.

"No, no," came her respectful voice. "You two make yourselves comfortable at the dining room table. I'll be right there." So we sat.

Rose had pulled her small table away from the one wall so we could all have equal access to the table. Orange candles were lit, and turkey-decorated napkins were wrapped around the silverware. Pickles, dinner rolls and butter along with gravy and mashed potatoes covered the center of the table. The rest of the food was situated on the birchbark coffee table: stuffing, sweet potatoes, corn and green beans.

"Here we are," Rose said as she finally joined us. She set the meat platter on the coffee table as well. "Would you mind if we say a small prayer of thanks before we eat?" Margaret and I both let her know that we had no problem with that.

After the prayer was said, Rose got up and went to the coffee table to retrieve the meat tray. I assumed we were having turkey, but there were two types of meat on the platter. I must've raised my eyebrows when the meat was handed off to me because the Indian woman quickly said, "Deer meat. I get plenty of it so eat all you want."

I handed the meat to Margaret, and then stood and helped Rose slide her chair in. "Thank you, Matt."

"Your welcome," I said and sat back down.

My neighbor took her share of potatoes and meat and passed them on. "So Matt, what did you do with yourself yesterday? Were you bored?"

I looked up from my plate and said, "Well, I slept late for one thing. Rita and I had gotten together the night before and stayed out quite late." Margaret smiled. at the mention of my girlfriend's name.

Before I could continue she interjected, "As the younger generation likes to say, Rose, she's Matt's main squeeze."

I nodded and then continued my story. "And I also took advantage of the motel's swimming pool and hot tub. Plus there's a nice size game room so I shot a couple rounds of pool with myself. Later, I looked through the notes I had put together on the other case I'm working on, hoping to find a link."

Margaret again, "This dog of a husband left his wife and kids and took all the money. What kind of man could do that?"

"In this day and age, plenty," Rose replied politely. "Speaking of missing links, something did come to mind while I slept the other night."

I almost jumped out of my chair. Did Rose actually have information I could use? "You did? What exactly did you remember?"

My neighbor scrambled ahead of her. "You have to wait, Matt. I made Rose promise not to tell you until we have dessert."

I placed my fork across my plate and pressed both hands, palms down, on the food-laden table. "Come on, ladies. Do I really have to wait that long?"

Margaret pleaded with her friend who was sitting across the table from her. "Don't do it, Rose. He'll shift gears and forget all about the nice Thanksgiving dinner sitting in front of him. He does it all the time."

"Sorry, Matt, a bargain is a bargain. Besides," Rose continued, "Margaret's been my friend for over twenty years, and I don't want to see that disappear. You'll see. Rewards come to those who wait." She picked up the potatoes and gravy bowl and offered them to me. "Here, I think you could use some more of this on your plate."

# CHAPTER 37

▼

In retrospect, it was well worth waiting for dessert. The women were right. Serving up sweets and answers at the same time was a great idea. Rose Jenson, also known as Running Water to her people, packaged the wandering Mandan issue up so neatly while we finished off her pumpkin pie, I felt I was given an early holiday present. As a matter of fact, if it had been closer to Christmas, I myself would've typed up my findings, placed the papers in a nice tight decorated box, and presented the gift to the Anoka-Hennepin School Board at its December meeting.

Yup, about a dozen or so people will be standing in line wanting to speak with me when we get back to the Twin Cities. Now if only I could tie up the loose ends concerning the elusive Brad Harper that quickly.

It wasn't until we crossed the state lines between North Dakota and Minnesota that Margaret and I finally discussed the wonderful Indian love story that Rose had shared with us. It had to be true, because so many of the puzzle pieces fit together. Of course, with the information we had gleaned, the scientists would want to run more tests before they stated the obvious.

"I'm sure glad I met your friend, Rose. That was some tale she had for us. A Mandan who couldn't take his eyes off a Sioux. According to her story, Chief Running Bear's son, Little Bear, fell madly in love with a beautiful Indian maiden in the spring of 1882. She was a member of the same Sioux tribe that was escorted out of Minnesota after the Sioux Uprising of 1862."

Margaret reached for her crocheting. She had gotten quite a bit finished since I dropped her off at her friend's. "Ah, huh. The two didn't get to stay together for long though, did they? The Indian maiden's chief decided his group should try going back to Minnesota that fall. His scouts had informed him that other Sioux had already crossed the land and gone back to the area they once knew."

I turned my head to the left to make sure there wasn't a car in my blind spot. None. I put on my blinkers and slowly shifted lanes. "Oh! Look at that Margaret. Three deer on my side coming out of those clusters of pine trees."

She shifted her body so she had a good view. "Such lovely creatures, aren't they?"

I nodded. "Until they run in front of a car or get hunted down. I imagine those three are scavenging for food now that the storm's blown over."

"Considering the time of day, you're probably right."

"Say, speaking of storm—I found Rose's addition of weather conditions for the time frame of her story, very interesting."

"That information would be significant, wouldn't it? Let's see, something about bad weather having started the middle of December that year. What were her exact words now?" Margaret tapped her forehead lightly. "Oh, yes, 'blizzard followed blizzard that year'."

The mere thought of a blizzard chilled me through and through. I raised the heat in the car just a tad. "Remember the phone call I made from your place that one night?"

"Why, of course. That's the same evening I called Rose."

"Well, my call was made to the main library in downtown Minneapolis. I asked a research gal to find out what kind of weather Minnesota was having in January of 1883."

My neighbor scooted her body up as straight as the car seat would allow, and then she excitedly asked, "What did you find out?"

"Minnesota had a couple blizzards in early and mid-January of that year."

Margaret dropped a stitch when she heard my reply. "Poor Little Bear. The town of Oak Grove was the end of the line for him. Never found the woman of his dreams. Near starvation. And then someone confronts him with a knife and his life is over. How sad."

"Isn't it," I said in a mellow tone.

"Matt, do you think he died because he was caught stealing from a farmer's cold storage food stash?"

"Beats me," I said as I pulled into a rest stop, "but wouldn't it be great if I could solve that crime, too?"

# CHAPTER 38

▼

Since our road trip took us so near the cut-off for my parents' house, Mrs. Grimshaw suggested that we stop and pick Gracie up now instead of my having to chase back there tomorrow. Not only would I be saving time but also gas.

Although Margaret's idea was a sound one, I thought she should be warned about the dog's ballistic nature whenever I'm out of her sight for more than a day, in case she wanted to change her mind. My neighbor simply shrugged her coat-covered shoulders and replied, "It won't bother me."

As we drew closer to the senior Malone household now, I was thankful that Minnesota wasn't hunkered down by the storm that raced through North Dakota the other day. With my father's ongoing recuperation from his untimely heart surgery, no one would've had the time to clear his driveway before we arrived. Cleaning that sucker in the winter can be a bear.

When I finally approached the area of tarred land set aside for cars on my folk's property, I tried to recall the last time there was no snow to speak of at Thanksgiving. Nothing came to mind. That revelation caused me to laugh internally, or so I thought that's all I did. But as soon as I saw Margaret's questioning glance, I knew I had actually snickered aloud. "Sorry, just thinking about something funny," I hastily explained. I should probably record this fact for prosperity. This was the first November visit ever that I didn't have to get the shovel out to free the Topaz from some entrapment.

"Care to share what passed through your brain cells a moment ago?"

"Oh, I'm just grateful that this lengthy path is fully exposed to the elements and as clean as glass, not thickly covered like it could have been if the snowstorm had hit this area."

Margaret quickly buttoned her coat and began sliding her gloves on while I rushed to set the brakes and shifted the car to park mode. Our plan was to get inside the house before the dog saw us and begged to be let out, but like all good plans there always seems to be a downfall. Mine was my cell phone.

Just as I cracked my door open, it began ringing. I immediately pulled the door shut and reached in my coat pocket where the phone was residing at the moment. Once the phone was firmly in my hand, I stared at the number being displayed on the tiny screen. The number wasn't familiar. I quickly turned towards my passenger and said, "It could be important. I think I better see who it is. Do you want me to turn the car back on for you?"

"No," Margaret replied. "I'm sure you won't be chatting that long."

So I pressed the send button which would connect me to the caller. "Matt Malone, how may I help you?" The reception was terrible. All I caught was something about Chubbs. That's what I get for buying a phone at deep discount. My brother's always nagging me about buying things at a higher rate if I want good quality, and I just keep ignoring him. Of course, he makes a six-figure income, while I on the other hand live on the fringes of unemployment almost weekly. I shouted into the phone as if that would resolve the problem. "I'll call you right back on a land phone, okay?" I never heard what the person's response was, but I ended the call. "Ready for the mutt, Margaret?"

"Ready," she replied gingerly.

I stepped out of the car, walked to the passenger door, and helped my neighbor out, and then I clutched her arm and started directing us to the house. "Brr … it's colder than I thought. I hope my folks have their fireplace on."

Just as I made that comment a gust of wind greeted us. It whirled around Margaret's head scarf and almost blew it away. She shivered. "Who was on the phone?"

We were almost to the door now. "Someone from the antique store in Elk River," I replied.

"Matt, dear, this is Thanksgiving, a major holiday. Why would someone be at the store?"

"Gosh, I don't know. I'm so exhausted I didn't even think about that." I reached for the handle. "Now remember what I told you. When Gracie comes running, just step to the side so she doesn't knock you down."

She shook her head. "I'll try my best."

As I predicted, Gracie came charging towards us. I placed my hand in front of me to stop her from crashing into us. "Get down, girl! You know better." Gracie hung her head and swiftly padded off behind me to Margaret, where she knew she'd get plenty of attention and no discipline.

Margaret scratched the back of the dog's ears. "Yes, that's a good girl. Nice girl." Gracie licked her hand.

Mom and Dad came from the kitchen to see what all the commotion was about. My mother spoke first. "Matt, what a nice surprise. We didn't expect to see you till tomorrow."

Because my father was standing at a different angle than my mother, he caught a glimpse of the guest I brought with. "And look who else is here."

Margaret stepped forward now. "Hello," she said in her soft sweet voice.

My mother strolled over to my travel mate and hugged her. "Oh, Mrs. Grimshaw. My goodness, it's been a long time since we've seen you. You're looking good." She turned her body a fraction to greet me, "Hi, honey," and kissed me on the cheek. "I hope you're not in a rush?"

I searched Margaret's eyes for an answer. "No, not really."

"Good," Dad said. "Let's go enjoy the fire in the livingroom."

Before my parents managed to usher me into the other room, I explained that I needed to use their house phone. Someone was waiting for me to return his call.

"Matt, why don't you use the one in the master bedroom," my mother suggested. "You'll have more privacy there."

"Thanks, I'll do that." I left the entryway and went down the hall to their sleeping quarters. The room smelled of Old Spice cologne and White Shoulder perfume. I shut the door quietly behind me, and then I ambled over to the oak night-stand and dialed the operator. "Yes, could you please connect me to Chubbs Antique Store in Elk River? Thank you."

While I waited for the call to be placed, I opened my wallet, took out a dollar and laid the bill on the table. The call was business related. I wasn't going to have my parents pick up my tab.

"Chubbs Antiques, Mary Allen speaking."

"Hello, Mary, this is Matt Malone. Someone just called me from your store, but we didn't talk long because of a bad connection. Would you happen to know who placed a call to me?"

Mary's tone sounded like she was displeased with my call. "Oh, of course. I'll tell him you're on the line." Then I heard her walk away from the phone.

Two minutes later, "Mister Malone," an out of breath male voice said on the other end. "I'm glad you understood who called you."

A chunk of my hair was covering my left eye so I combed my fingers through it and brushed it back on top of my head. "Well, I deciphered the word Chubbs and thought that was enough to go on."

A grunt and then, "That's why you're the PI, and I'm just a lowly salesperson," Glen Wilson said.

My head swelled considerably upon hearing the young man's nonsense. "If it makes you feel any better, I haven't figured out what you're doing at work on Thanksgiving."

"Oh, yeah, I suppose an outsider would wonder about that. You see the Friday after Thanksgiving we offer a big discount to the public just like all the regular stores in town. Well, since Mary and I didn't have anyone to share a meal with, we offered to come in this evening to shift inventory around and put up signs."

"Makes perfect sense to me," I said and then I yawned. "So what's happened at the antique store since I last saw you, Glen? Must be pretty darn important for you to track me down today of all days."

"Yes, sir, it is." The urgency in his tone rippled across the lines. "The same guy who sold me the candlesticks stopped by here last night right before closing."

"Really?"

"Yeah. Of course, he didn't look exactly the same, but there's no way I would ever forget his peculiar mannerisms or the deep color of his eyes."

"What was he trying to sell you this time?" I asked genuinely interested.

"Oh, I'm sorry if I mislead you. He didn't talk to me this time, I was working on the second level. Mary Allen was the one at the counter. But as soon as I heard his booming voice share that he wanted to sell some Indian artifacts he'd found on property he recently inherited, I knelt down and looked through the railing slots. Got an excellent view of him from that position."

Could this really be Harper or another false alarm? "Geez Glen, I just got back from a long road trip and I don't know when I'll be able to get back to up to Elk River to chat. Can you spare some time right now?"

"Sure. We've finished moving the stuff around and just have to attach new price tickets on some of the items. What do you want to talk about, Mr. Malone."

"Well, if you're sure Mary won't object to my taking you away from your work for a bit, I'd appreciate it if you could give me a detailed description of the guy who visited with her."

"No problem." Glen stopped speaking to me now to tell his co-worker he'd be off the phone in five minutes and to ask if she was all right with that. The female voice in the background told him to do whatever he needed to do. "Okay, I'm ready."

I smiled at myself in the dresser mirror, thinking about all the money I'd be collecting for closing two cases at once. "Go ahead, Glen. I'm all ears."

# CHAPTER 39

▼

With my phone conversation finally concluded now, I hummed a happy tune as I opened the door and headed down the hall to rejoin the others. That short chat with Glen fueled my optimistic mood. My hunch concerning Harper's location was already in place, but now the spot was nailed down tight, and I needed to act quickly before he split.

As I reached the Spanish archway leading from the entrance into the living room I stopped and took in the view. All the people I loved, minus one, were sitting together nice and cozy-like making small talk. Even Gracie expressed an opinion. A perfect Kodak moment or if you prefer paintings, I'd classify the scene as a Norman Rockwell. Nope, they're not going to be happy when I break my news to them.

Talk that had been freely flowing before my shoes comfortably rested on the carpet suddenly halted. It seemed that the focus of the people in room was entirely glued to me now. I suppose they were all probably expecting me to share some major revelation. Too bad it wouldn't be forthcoming. All I said was, "Sorry about that phone call, but it was extremely important."

My father chose to speak for the three of them. "We understand, Son. You don't need to apologize for not having a job that goes from nine to five like most people." He pushed himself off the couch and waved for me to come further into the room. "All that matters is that you're here now. Come and sit a spell." I obeyed knowing full well that I'd be leaving in a matter of minutes. The two chairs nearest the fireplace were vacant so I plopped myself in one, and my dad the other. Now he continued, "Mrs. Grimshaw already filled us in on what she did in Bismark, but why exactly did you go?"

I stole a glance at Margaret.

"Relax, Matt," she said in a reassuring tone. "I only told them what *I* did."

Her stressed *I* clued me in that she hadn't repeated what went on between Rose and us. Before I said anything, I signaled Gracie to join me for moral support. "I ... ah ... we really need to get going. It's way past Mrs. Grimshaw's bedtime." Appropriately timed but not at all planned, Margaret suddenly released a long yawn. "See," I pointed in her direction.

My parents looked from one to the other. Clearly they were disappointed. "Ah, Mom and Dad, I'll tell you about my trip another time. I promise. It's just too darn late tonight." It was a crumb, but it was something. I could've left them empty-handed.

Apparently my neighbor didn't buy my blarney even though she normally went to bed around this hour. She stopped yawning and said, "What's really going on, Matt? You can trust us."

"Okay!" I stood, braced my hands on my hips and then began pacing back and forth. "My stomach's doing those stupid flip-flops again."

Mom chimed in, "Are you referring to that lovely sixth sense you inherited?"

"Don't you mean curse, honey?" Dad added.

"Whatever!" I replied a little too harshly. "Anyway, I have this hunch I want to follow through on, and that means I need to rise fairly early. And, as you might remember, I've never done well at getting up before sunrise even in the Air Force. So I need to get to bed as soon as possible."

"Where are you going?" the three of them asked, acting like triplets.

"To Oak Grove."

My parents' faces clouded over. They didn't understand.

My traveling companion, who remained sitting, gave me a break and filled them in. "He's going to the property where the new middle school is being built."

"Matt, there is a solution to your problem," my mom said. "You two can stay overnight. We have plenty of room."

Dad interjected, "Yeah, besides our place is a heck of a lot closer to Oak Grove than yours."

I ran my hand through my hair, "Geez, I don't know." I was too tired to argue. "What do you think, Mrs. Grimshaw?"

She must've been on the verge of nodding off because her head jerked up so hard it almost snapped off. "Huh? What's that?"

"My folks just asked us to spend the night. Is that all right with you?"

She smiled weakly. "Yes, that would be lovely. I don't think I have any appointments in the morning."

"That's settled then," I said. "Mom, where did you hang my coat?"

My mother quickly asked, "Why?" and then rushed to the doorway to block it. I tried to edge around her medium-sized frame, but she stood her ground. We were eyeball to eyeball now. "Matt, Mrs. Grimshaw just said she was fine with staying."

I slapped my hands against my legs. "So she did, but I think she'd prefer to slip into her bed clothes, don't you?"

Mom must've been pretty tired herself because she didn't catch my drift.

Dad calmly moved me aside. "Dear, I think what Matt is trying to say is that their suitcases are still in the car." I nodded. "I'll get your coat."

"Thanks, Dad."

Mom freed up the archway, and we stepped through.

"Say, Mom, is that mind reading thing another hidden talent the Malone family has? Because I'd benefit more from that one."

She laughed. "No, Son. It's something that can only be acquired after raising children or being married for many years."

"Darn! That leaves me out."

# CHAPTER 40

▼

The alarm went off at 6:00 A.M. sharp. I hurriedly pushed my lazy body to a sitting position and shut the buzzer off. Then I sat up, reached for my tee shirt and jeans that I'd left at the foot of the bed the night before, and quickly slipped into them. Since it was so early in the morning, I debated whether to put shoes on for about one second but opted against it. As far as I knew bare feet still weren't known to make any noise and therefore I wouldn't have to tiptoe passed the other occupied bedrooms as I made my way to the kitchen on the other side of the house.

Of course, when I reached the kitchen I discovered it didn't matter if I'd worn loud clunky shoes or ballet slippers on the hallway's hardwood floors because not one, but three very sleepy faces were sitting at the kitchen table solemnly staring at me as I quietly entered the room. Each person was stylishly wrapped in their own warm weather bathrobe and held a cup of steaming, freshly brewed coffee in their hands.

I said, "Good-morning," softly, not wanting to shatter the noise level yet and then went directly to the cupboard for a cup. When I got what I wanted, I padded over to the coffeepot to fill it and said, "Care if I join the three of you?"

"Sure, sure," Dad answered lazily, "pull up a chair. There's plenty of room for you."

As soon as I dragged a chair out from under the table, my mother yawned and said, "No one seems to be ready for breakfast yet, Matt, but if you'd like me to whip something up for you before you leave, I'd be happy to do it."

I set my coffee cup on the table across from my mother. "Ah, no thanks. That won't be necessary, Mom. I thought I'd just make myself a couple pieces of toast. You do have plenty of bread, right?"

My mother's head was bent down as she busily stirred her coffee with a teaspoon. She must've just added sugar, I thought. She always likes her morning libations to be extra sweet. Without looking up from what she was doing, she replied, "Yes, we have a loaf of wheat and one of white." She shifted her position enough that her chair scrapped the floor, indicating she was about to get up.

"Stay put, Mom," I said. "I can get it."

"All right, but I don't keep the bread in the bread box anymore. You'll find it on the bottom shelf of the fridge."

The kitchen was small so I didn't have to use too much energy to get from the table to the fridge. I opened the door and bent down to retrieve a couple slices of wheat bread. While I was in this position, my father decided to bring something to my attention. "Matt, the three of us have been talking about your mission today. The ladies think I should ride shotgun with you, not literally but metaphorically speaking, in case you run into trouble of some sort."

I straightened my body, closed the fridge door, and then placed two slices of bread in the toaster. After I was finished with that, I swung around towards the table and said, "Look, I appreciate your concern, but I honestly don't foresee any difficulties. If I'm wrong, well, I'd rather know that Dad's back here in the safety of his own home." My father leaned back in his chair and crossed his arms. "You've already gone through so much this year, Dad. I would never forgive myself if you got injured in anyway, nor would my siblings."

My father came on a bit defensive but not as strong as I expected. "Just for the record, Matt, I can still handle any problems that arise."

"I know you can, Dad, just not today. I mean it!" Now I glanced around the room and noticed someone was missing. "Anyone seen Gracie?"

"Outside. She couldn't sleep either," Margaret replied. "She knew she had to do her thing. That's why I'm up so early."

"I'm sorry she woke you. That mutt must've snuck out of my room during the night."

"It's okay," Margaret said. "I decided to tackle my crocheting project while everyone was still asleep."

"Well, since Gracie's already outside, just leave her out there. I plan to take her with me."

"Now you're playing smart, Matt," my neighbor said in a satisfied tone.

My toast popped up. I put it on a plate and spread peanut butter on both pieces. "What? My bringing the dog? I planned on doing that since last night." Now I brought my plate to the table and sat. "I figured Gracie would enjoy running free on the school property. It's such a huge piece of land."

Margaret nodded. "That's for sure, but there won't be as much open space once everything is developed."

Dad finished off his coffee so now he got up and took his cup over to the counter by the sink where he always stashes it for later use. "Well, if no one minds, I think I'm going to go back to bed for a while." He left the counter and started out of the kitchen

"Okay," I said. "I'll see you in a couple hours."

"All right," he replied sleepily as he continued down the hall.

"Mrs. Grimshaw, would you like another cup of coffee?" my mother politely asked.

"Yes, that would be nice," she replied in a low voice. "Mrs. Malone, how is your husband really doing? I've never had the opportunity to ask you."

After my mother handed Margaret her refill, she sat down again. "It's very kind of you to ask. The doctor says he's progressing nicely. You know earlier you mentioned my husband's weight loss. That's actually a good sign."

"It is?" I said as I munched on my toast.

Mom took a sip of coffee. "Of course it is. That means he's been really watching what he eats. And the naps—that's normal too. It takes quite awhile for the body to get back up to speed." As she bent her head down towards her coffee cup now, she dropped her voice. "The main thing doctors worry about after someone has had heart surgery is depression."

Margaret leaned back in her chair and clutched her chest. "Oh, my. I didn't realize one fell into depression after heart surgery."

"Yup," I interrupted. "It's a very mental thing. Since my father had his surgery, I've read tons of books on the subject. Because a person's body takes so long to heal and people aren't allowed to do or eat the things they used to, they start feeling sorry for themselves. I imagine the medication they are given is partly to blame too."

Saying that, I became bothered by what I said to my father only a few minutes ago. I looked into my mother's eyes. "Mom, do you think I upset Dad by telling him I didn't want him to come along?"

She placed her coffee-warm hand over mine. "Matt, don't you go thinking like that. Your father was so tired. I'm sure he was glad that you didn't need him. Besides, it was Margaret's and my idea, not his."

When she took her hand off mine I glanced at my wristwatch. Thirty minutes had passed since I stepped into the kitchen. I shoved my chair back. "Well, if you ladies will excuse me, I really do need to hit the road."

The two women wished me well and said they'd see me later.

# CHAPTER 41

▼

Since I had been out to the school property previously, I was familiar with two different ways of getting there. Today I chose the easiest route, the one I used for the groundbreaking ceremony.

Gracie was so happy to be riding alongside me, and believe me, she let me know it every chance she got. Normally when we're at home her demeanor is on the lazy side, but that changes as soon as she steps foot in a car. She's up; she's down; then she's up again. Right now her behavior was off any chart for normal. Going bonkers was a better way to describe her activity. I suppose the mixture of her thinking she was heading home plus all the little critters running amok in front of her made her more excitable this particular trip.

Anyway, after driving for approximately fifteen minutes with an out-of-control dog, I finally decided I had enough and needed to remedy the situation. I eased my right hand off the wheel and patted the dog on the head. Not hard mind you. Just a gentle tap. "Calm down, girl. It's not too much longer now. As soon as we get to the woods, you can chase those squirrels all you want."

Gracie graciously accepted the attention she was receiving from her master by licking my face clean. After she finished with me, she swung her head towards the passenger window to see what she had missed. Of course when her rump came around my way, I was immediately pelted with her large bushy matted tail. Great! Now her wagging tail was as huge a distraction as her previous standing and sitting were. Nothing like having an accident on the way to solving a case. "Sit," I commanded her in an irritated tone. Then I applied firm pressure on the center of her back. She obeyed and sat for about four seconds.

What a waste of time. It looks like I'm going to have to put up with a wild dog whether I want to or not. I returned my right hand to the steering wheel, positioned it in the correct four o'clock position, and tuned my mind to the business I'd be handling in just a matter of minutes.

What's the best way to approach my prey, I wondered. I don't want him to bolt as soon as he sees me coming. Perhaps I should drive one block past Flamingo Way and park on the other side of the woods.

As I crossed the street the school site was located on, I glanced down the road in that direction. "Yup, just as I suspected. The man I was hunting was already hard at work. The street I planned to park on was next, so I took a left turn and stopped midway through the street.

Now that I had arrived at my destination, the closer I came to meeting up with the man I planned on confronting, the less I exuded the confidence I shared with everyone around the breakfast table. It would be nice to have some sort of protection I thought, like a gun. But since I don't carry one, a different venue would be necessary.

I turned the ignition off, but I wasn't quite ready to head for the woods yet. The more I mulled over everything that could go wrong the more I was certain I needed a backup plan. So I whipped out my cell phone and placed a call to my friend Sgt. Murchinak; a short time later I'd be extremely thankful for that call. Sgt. Murchinak wasn't picking up so I left a voice message. When I was done I hung up and tossed the cell phone back in the glove compartment where I had found it.

Now I was ready. I zipped up my winter jacket and then put Gracie on her leash and got out of the car. I'd unhook the dog once we were on the school property.

It was a good thing that it was nearly winter, for most of the leaves were off the trees, and it was easy to see exactly where the boundaries were for the new school. I gave Gracie a signal, and she minded my silent cue perfectly.

The CAT operator, Ron, never heard us approaching. By the time he finally sensed someone was near, he could have been flattened to a pulp. His butt was up in the air, and his head and arms were extended into a hole searching for something. I presumed it was for more antiques, but I could be wrong.

"Hey, what are you digging for, Ron? I thought this place was off limits till the Indians decided if this land's a burial site or not?"

I startled him, and he hastily sat back on his haunches. "Oh, it's only you." Obviously my appearance didn't frighten him. Now he placed his hands on his knees. They were filthy from digging. "I could ask the same of you," he replied sarcastically.

I ignored the way he responded. "And my answer would be the same as last time," I said. "Just driving through."

He looked at the curbing along the street. "So then where's your car?"

"I came through there," I said as I pointed towards the woods behind him. "I have my dog along with me today, and I thought she'd enjoy chasing down squirrels."

Ron acted like he didn't trust my answer and he began scanning the premises. When he reached 180 degrees, he finally caught a glimpse of Gracie. "That your dog over there?"

"Yup, that's her. Sometimes she rides with me when I have a short job to do." I stared at him coldly. "So you gonna tell me what you're looking for?"

He stood almost to his full height and tried to rub the gritty dirt from his hands. "I think I lost my knife when we lifted the skeleton out of the hole."

"Hmm? I jumped back in there right after we took the skeleton out, and I sure didn't see anything." I drew my eyes to my wristwatch. "Tell you what, I'm in no hurry, and the dog's enjoying herself. How about if I offer you a hand?"

I think I was too eager to help. Ron looked at me suspiciously. "Nah, that's all right. I probably just misplaced it at home somewhere."

"And where exactly would home be, Mr. Harper?" I bravely asked.

Ron scowled so hard at me he could've burned a hole through my heart.

"What's wrong? Your legal name is Brad Harper, isn't it?"

"What the ...?" The Paul Bunyan look-alike hoisted his frame to full stature, took a running start and slammed into my body head on. The force of the blow was so hard I thought he had cracked all my ribs. I laid there in agony.

Now generally speaking, when someone attacks another person they either want to kill you or knock you unconscious. Either way, they'd have to give you many blows to the head or body to accomplish that feat. So while Ron was deciding what his next move would be, I planned my own defense strategy. As soon as he leans over me, I'll kick him where the sun doesn't shine. That ought to give me time to move out of his way.

But my planning was off kilter. Ron walked behind me instead, and stood near my head. From his new position now, he jerked my arms back and started dragging me to the open six-foot-deep hole. I struggled the best I could, but it was no use. If I tried any harder I felt my arms would be pulled from their sockets.

Gracie bounded up finally to see what was going on. She sniffed us both and then pawed playfully at Harper's pants. Darn! She thought we were playing. So much for security.

Ron Girard, A.K.A. Brad Harper, opened his mouth before tossing me in the pit. "Who the heck sent you? Violet?"

I didn't respond.

Apparently he wasn't going to ask me again. He straddled his large frame over the opening and let go of me. My butt smacked the hard earth first. Even though I ached from head to toe, I appreciated the fact that my derriere was well padded. Real swift Malone, the jerk outsmarted you. Now how are you going to get out of this mess? Before I could think of anything, dirt was rapidly toppling down around me. Pictures of me being buried alive suddenly flashed through my head. Would my skeleton be uncovered in another hundred years like the Indian we found?

Brad Harper started yelling at me as he added more dirt. "You know I have nothing to lose. My wife hasn't a clue where I am, and no one at work knows anything about the real me."

Then he laughed like the devil. "It's like I'm a ghost. I can go anywhere and do anything I want." Then he tossed another load of dirt into the hole.

Just as I began to wonder where the heck the calvary was when you needed them, Gracie released a shrill bark, and I heard an unfamiliar voice say, "Okay, mister, put your hands up where we can see them and then turn around slowly. That's right. Now move this way one step at a time. Keep on coming." The speaker coughed. Okay, Mitchell, pat him down, and then handcuff him and read him his rights."

A lone Oak Grove policeman, who looked like a fresh recruit, quickly squatted near the edge of the hole I was in and peered down at me. "You all right, Mr. Malone?"

I couldn't say much at first. I was coughing too much from all the dirt that had been piled on me. When I finally thought my lungs were cleared I said, "So, so," and then I began coughing again. Since that wasn't all I wanted to say to the young cop, I took a deep breath and then rushed on with the rest. "But I'll be feeling a lot better once you get me out of here and help me catch that dumb mutt of mine."

# EPILOGUE

▼

## Nine Months Later

Most of us are familiar with the old adage, *killing two birds with one stone.* Of course, if you're anything like me, you've never given it much thought. Well, this past year I finally got around to considering the true meaning of the words when I wound up doing it myself. In my updated version no birds were involved although I know of one particular one I'd like to get rid of, but I digress. Sorry. I simply solved two cases with one shard of pottery. Mrs. Harper was happy her man was behind bars, and Little Bear's remains were shipped back to his people for proper Indian burial.

Remember my old friend Professor Ted Raines? He reconnected with me super fast the moment the publicity hit all the news' venues. We've met a couple times since that conversation via the phone. Our first visit together didn't go that smoothly because, frankly, Ted was upset that I didn't share my thoughts concerning the Indian skeleton. But how could I do that? I needed to solve the riddle and also rake in some dough. If I would've told him, my job would've been history. Anyway, after his inflated feelings got reshaped, we were finally able to sit down like two civilized people and partake of information as well as food. This occurred on a hot August day in Dinkytown over the lunch hour.

"You know, Ted, I still can't believe that my two cases were joined at the hip." My friend was kind enough to acknowledge my comment before taking a bite of his quarter-pound hamburger he had ordered. He nodded his head in agreement. "After the Oak Grove Police reined in Brad Harper at the police station, my old buddy from a downtown precinct, Sgt. Murchinak, gleaned plenty of tidbits for me. According to him, Brad Harper's great-grandfather once owned land that was butted up against the Cox's farm.

"He must've been out in his field checking on his cattle, with the weather conditions the way they were, and along comes half-starved Little Bear riding through his land on horseback." I took a few fries from their boxed packaging material and slathered them with ketchup. Then I placed them in my mouth.

Ted patted his large mouth with a small paper napkin again. It seemed like every time he took a bite of hamburger, ketchup and mustard oozed out. But this was his final clean-up job; I could tell he was preparing to share his thoughts now. "And don't forget, he was probably remembering how his mother died at the hands of Indians when he was just a young lad living in Iowa. Scared, he panicked and reached for his Smith and Wesson Bowie knife that he happened to be carrying on him. His awful childhood memories dangled in front of him like a matador's red cape. How could he not react like an angry bull? After he knocked the half-starved Mandan Indian off the horse, he plunged his knife straight into the Indian's heart."

"Crazy, ain't it," is all I managed to say as I shoved two more fries into my mouth. "An Indian maiden's departure wounded a brave's heart. His heart won't mend so he takes off to search her out in an unknown land, only to die from a wound to the heart by a white man's hand."

Finished with our lunches now, Ted waved for the waitress to bring our check. "So Matt," he said, "when exactly did you suspect that Ron Girard was Brad Harper?"

I pushed my empty plate aside and leaned on the table. "I think I started to become suspicious when Harper's arms were slightly exposed. He rushed to cover them up too quickly. Luckily, he didn't realize that I had already caught a glimpse of what appeared to be a tattoo of some sort."

The waitress finally came with our bill, and we divided the payment equally.

"I presume that happened when you two were carrying the skeleton from the hole." Ted took his wallet out and placed the amount he owed on the tiny black plastic server's payment tray.

I already had my money out so I tossed it on there too. "Yup," I replied. I carefully returned my wallet to my back pocket.

With our meal paid for now, we didn't dawdle much longer. We just stood, shook hands, and promised not to wait several years to get together again. The very last comment Ted Raines shared with me was to complain that his afternoon was shot as he was returning to the college campus to give his summer students an exam. I told him not to feel too bad. I had the good fortune of chauffeuring three women, over forty, to Oak Grove in my old Topaz.

I always planned to stop at my girlfriend's first because she lived closer to Din-kytown and the University of Minnesota, but now I began to wonder if that was such a good idea. Rita doesn't like being overly hot in the summertime, and while I was enjoying lunch, the temperature in the car had risen sharply, and there wasn't sufficient time for the air-conditioner to reduce it.

I smiled as I pulled up to the curbing where Rita's apartment building stands. I fretted for nothing. Rita Sinclair, my honey, was dressed accordingly. She wore a sleeveless red sun dress and new black sandals. Her dark hair was pulled back tight and pinned up, and red heart-shaped earrings dangled from her tiny ear-lobes. The ruby-red lipstick she used to paint her luscious lips really showed off her merry mouth.

After my sweetheart arranged herself in the front passenger car seat, she noted that I was dressed appropriately also. "No suit, huh? I can't blame you," she said. "Uncle Harold warned me that the school's air-conditioning unit wasn't up and running yet. It's too bad they couldn't have put the dedication ceremony off till a cooler day, like say in September."

I released my right hand from the steering wheel and waved it at her. "Septem-ber can be pretty unbearable too, or have you forgotten? Now, if we were only meeting in the basement," I said, "we'd be plenty cool. An article that recently ran in the Star Tribune stated that over 300,000 concrete blocks were used to build the new middle school."

"300,000 blocks!" Rita folded her hands in her lap. "I can't even picture that amount in my head. You know there's always some sort of construction going on downtown near where I work, but I've never actually taken the time to look through one of those peepholes provided for the curious layperson. I guess I'll have to stop and see what all the fuss is about the next time a new building begins cropping up."

I laughed. "You really haven't missed much. The foundation is just a bunch of rectangles made from cement, stacked on top of each other and glued together with mixed cement, most of which is hidden below ground level." Then I had an idea. "Hey, tell you what, the next house my brother Jim builds, I'll take you by the site and you can see what the guts of a house look like."

"Promise?," my girlfriend said as she twisted her hands a little.

I took my right hand off the steering wheel for a moment and held it up as if I was taking an oath on the witness stand. "I solemnly promise."

"Hello," I'm Evan Cox. "Some of you might recall seeing me at the ground-breaking ceremony. Of course, at that time, the school board, some politicians and I were seated on a platform outside, overlooking the area which now is your new school. This past year has been quite an adventure for me as well as for your school board members. We watched a new school transform before our very eyes. The school's beginnings were only a simple hole in the ground and then as if by magic it literally shaped into what it is today. Isn't it amazing what can get accomplished in such a short time?" Evan asked with great pride.

Cheering, whistling, feet stomping, and clapping immediately flooded the auditorium.

"I ask that all of you take a good look at this new building before you leave the premises this afternoon. As you wander the halls and classrooms later, take note of the building's structure. There are 700 doors and window frames, as well as 5000 light fixtures. And please, don't forget to look at the program you were handed as you entered this magnificent school. It acknowledges the seventy vendors who helped create the school you've only dreamed about. Some of those people are sitting among you today." Evan scanned the audience. "Why don't you stand, so we can give you a proper thank you."

Twenty or so men and women stood, and then the audience clapped and yelled, "Yay." The workers accepted the ovations for two minutes before Evan finally motioned for silence.

"Now I'd like to get serious if I may. In just a little while, we will be uncovering the bust of the person your school has been named after. I want you to know that the task of naming a school is not taken lightly. The district you live in mandates that a school be named in honor of a prominent dead person or the geographic area that will be served by the school." Evan turned slightly and gave the president of the board a small wave. "Thanks to Carolyn's persuasion," she raised her hooked hand to him, "the new school is not being named after the many oak groves found throughout this community. It is being named after a Native American.

"You know, even though it's almost the twenty-first century, many people still find it difficult to think of Indians as part of our culture. I've often wondered why." Mr. Cox pulled out another piece of paper and slipped it on top of what he just read. "In a book I just finished reading, the author states that as early as the seventeenth century, European explorers noted that most of our ideas of self-government and democracy came from the Indian's thoughts on freedom. Now isn't that interesting? Since the seventeenth century we've gleaned ideas from the Indians.

"Well, I can tell you this. Your new school is never going to forget one very special Indian. The school has been named after Little Bear, a Mandan Indian who died with honor. For those of you who don't know much about Native American Indians, the Mandan were a friendly, semi-nomadic tribe who once roamed freely in North Dakota, intermingling with other Siouan tribes.

"Like Little Bear, who struggled with diversity and new challenges in his movements in North Dakota and his journey to Minnesota, a child's education is a long journey which exposes them to diversity and many new experiences too, some more challenging than others.

"Today I place a challenge before your children, our future. Be the first to seek out diversity in the people you surround yourself with and in your reading material—for it is in so doing that you gain knowledge of yourselves as well as others, and in this way you can relate better to your fellow man."

Carolyn Sorenson's two-piece off-white suit really showed off her svelte figure as she strolled over to the podium to join Evan now. His speech was finally over. It was long like he predicted at the groundbreaking ceremony, but he had some great things to say, and it went straight to the heart. I really hoped the kids were listening.

The president of the board put her good hand on Evan's shoulder. "Mr. Cox, thank you so much for that wonderful speech. On behalf of the school board and the middle school parents, I want to thank you once again for your generous help in getting this middle school built." Evan nodded humbly as I've seen him do before. Then he took his seat alongside Rita's Uncle Harold, the other board members and dignitaries.

"Our next guest," Carolyn said, "is Rose Running Water Jenson, a member of the Mandan Hidasta tribe. Ms. Jenson lived in Minnesota for a brief time and currently lives in Bismark, North Dakota." Mrs. Grimshaw's silver-haired friend walked to the podium, and then Carolyn returned to her seat.

I'm sure some people were disappointed by what Rose, a Native American wore, but I wasn't. She only wears her jingle dress for pow wows and other Indian ceremonies. This was not an Indian function so she wore only her Sunday best, a long navy-blue dress with three-quarter length sleeves and black Mary Jane shoes. Her ears and neck however were adorned with a beaded necklace and earrings made by one of her people.

As I mentioned earlier Rose is a small woman, but today she appeared to be about nine-feet tall. "Good afternoon. On behalf of the Mandan Hidasta people I want to thank you for honoring a young Mandan Indian brave. When Little Bear wandered through this part of Minnesota during a January blizzard of 1883, he was only in the winter of his eighteenth year, the same age as most high school seniors. Why did he leave his family and come to Oak Grove you might ask?

According to stories that have been passed down to me, he left North Dakota to seek the inner peace he was missing. His first love, a Sioux Indian, had moved back to Minnesota with her tribe in the fall of 1882. Unfortunately he died on this very property before he found his true love, or as we say nowadays his soul-mate.

I'd like to take you back now to a time long before Little Bear even existed. "In the year 1852, Chief Seattle wrote a letter to President Franklin Pierce in which he said, 'The earth does not belong to man, man belongs to the earth. All things are connected.... Man did not weave the web of life, he is merely a strand in it. Whatever he does to the web he does to himself'.

"I ask that you remember what Chief Seattle said, my dear students and teachers. You have a wonderful environmental lab available to you in the glorious woods and pond behind your school. I encourage you to study the flora and fauna—through them you will learn many things about the earth and how it interacts with us.

"Now children, entering this new school, I have a special Mandan message for you, xo-ka-na-k-da (behave yourself)." All of the adults in the audience laughed when we heard Rose's English version.

*　　*　　*　　*

"Great speech, Rose," I said as the four of us walked out of the school building together.

"Thank you, Matt."

"My, my, it looks like we're in for a weather change," Mrs. Grimshaw said. Then she linked her arm with her ex-neighbor and they stepped onto the sidewalk that led to the parking lot. Rita followed close behind.

Margaret was right. The air smelled different, and the sun wasn't shining anymore even though we had plenty of daylight ahead of us. I stopped walking and glanced up at the sky to see what was happening. Dark storm clouds were brewing, but that wasn't the only activity I caught high above our heads. Two huge birds were soaring over the middle school campus also.

The gals, Rita, Margaret and Rose, were in such deep conversation they were missing the show. "Ladies," I yelled. The three women were still talking when they turned towards me. I pointed to the birds, and a hush finally fell over them. Now while we silently stared at the eagles, the birds that are still revered by Native Americans today, I wondered if Little Bear had come to bless the school named after him and to perhaps thank us for reuniting him with his kin.

But of course, after the magic of the moment was over, I didn't dare share my masculine thoughts aloud. Instead, I simply showered the ears of the women surrounding me with romantic mush. I knew that's what they would prefer to hear, "Well, it looks like Little Bear, our North Dakota neighbor, and his true love have found each other at last."

978-0-595-47893-4
0-595-47893-X

CPSIA information can be obtained
at www.ICGtesting.com
Printed in the USA
FFHW021618050619
52852072-58400FF